No one "foils" Nancy Drew...

"This is DeLyn and Damon Brittany," George went on. "Nancy, Ned, and my cousin Bess."

"Glad to meet you," Damon said with a smile and a hearty handshake.

DeLyn stuck out her hand too, but she didn't speak, and her smile struck me as pretty forced. Why? I wondered. Pre-match nerves, maybe.

We stood there for a minute, chatting about the tournament. I noticed DeLyn's distracted gaze sliding away, scanning the parking lot. I looked around too.

That's when I spotted him, lingering behind a parked car two rows away, like he was waiting for someone. A guy with shaggy, shoulder-length brown hair and a restless way of moving that raised my radar.

NANCY DREW
girl detective™

Available from Aladdin Paperbacks

NANCY DREW

DREW
girl detective ™

#17

En Garde

CAROLYN KEENE

Aladdin Paperbacks
New York   London   Toronto   Sydney

❧ ALADDIN PAPERBACKS
An imprint of Simon & Schuster Children's Publishing Division
1230 Avenue of the Americas, New York, NY 10020
Copyright © 2006 by Simon & Schuster, Inc.
All rights reserved, including the right of
reproduction in whole or in part in any form.
NANCY DREW is a registered trademark of Simon & Schuster, Inc.
ALADDIN PAPERBACKS, NANCY DREW: GIRL DETECTIVE, and colophon are trademarks of Simon & Schuster, Inc.
Manufactured in the United States of America
First Aladdin Paperbacks edition May 2006
10 9 8 7
Library of Congress Control Number 2005929098
ISBN-13: 978-1-4169-0603-2
ISBN-10: 1-4169-0603-7

Contents

En Garde

Tournament Time

Let me tell you about George Fayne. To start with, she's my best friend—one of them, at least. And she's a she, no matter what her name says. (Her real name is Georgia, but don't tell her I told you.)

Oh, my name? I'm Nancy Drew. Maybe you've heard of me. I've solved a few mysteries around River Heights, but it's no big deal. Seriously. It's not like I even go looking for cases. They just sort of . . . find me.

Besides, I don't do it alone. And one of the people who helps me out the most is my friend George. She's always there for me when I need her. So when George does something on her own, I support her. Even if I don't entirely understand her. Like right now, for instance.

"So you think she's going to stick with this fencing thing?" I asked Bess as we got out of my car.

(Oh, yeah, Bess Marvin is my other best friend/partner in crime solving. She's George's cousin, and the three of us go way back.)

"I actually think she will," Bess said, flipping her wavy golden hair out of her jacket collar. "This just may be her sport."

"George is good at every sport she tries," said my boyfriend, Ned Nickerson. "Basketball, cycling, rock climbing, skiing, scuba diving, you name it."

"This is different," said Bess. "Her coach says she's really good at fencing, and it sounds so intense. He says once you commit to it, it's got to be a full-time thing. That's all you hear from her these days—it's 'Bela says this' and 'Bela says that.'"

"That's what I don't get," Ned said. "That coach. Who'd want to spend so much time with that guy?"

I couldn't help laughing as we walked across the parking lot. "You take a two-day fencing workshop and suddenly you have an enemy for life. What *did* that man do to you?" I asked.

Ned grinned back, but he stuck to his point. "It was so brutal. Every move I made, Bela Kovacs said it was totally wrong. The way he kept sniping at me, I felt so clumsy."

"Your fencing looked fine in that Shakespeare

2

play," I reassured him. "That's why you took the workshop, right?"

"Yup, I went through two long, grueling days of torture so I could learn enough fencing to do three minutes of stage dueling," Ned agreed. "George came along to keep me company, and now she's hooked for life. It's all my fault!" He pretended to plunge a dagger into his heart and then staggered dramatically for a few steps.

"Shhh, there she is," Bess warned us, as she waved across the parking lot.

Standing in front of the University of River Heights field house, I could spot George's short dark hair, the ends spiky and mussed as always. Usually George is the tallest girl in any group, but the girl she stood next to now was just as tall, with elegant, erect posture. The same was true of the guy they were standing with. Seeing them, I self-consciously straightened my own shoulders. All three were dressed in white—flat white shoes, white knee socks, white knickers, and white turtlenecks. The dazzling white outfits were particularly striking against George's friends' dark African-American skin. They looked impressive, I had to say.

"That must be DeLyn and her twin brother," Bess said as we hurried to join George and her companions. "George is always talking about them. They're supposed to be fabulous fencers. They've studied with Kovacs for years."

"I remember seeing them around the salle—that's what fencers call the studio where they train," Ned said. "The twins are incredible. I hope we get the chance to watch them fence today, too."

"Hi, guys!" George called out to us. "I'm so glad you're here."

"Hey, you can't have your first fencing match without your regular cheering section," I declared.

George grinned nervously, pulling her bulky equipment bag onto her shoulder. "Well, this won't count toward national ranking—it's just an informal meet. But Bela says it'll be good for me to get some bout experience."

At the words "Bela says," Bess flashed me an I-told-you-so look. Good thing George didn't notice, since I could hardly keep from giggling.

"This is DeLyn and Damon Brittany," George went on. "Nancy, Ned, and my cousin Bess."

"Glad to meet you," Damon said with a smile and a hearty handshake.

DeLyn stuck out her hand too, but she didn't speak, and her smile struck me as pretty forced. Why? I wondered. Pre-match nerves, maybe.

We stood there for a minute, chatting about the tournament. I noticed DeLyn's distracted gaze sliding

4

away, scanning the parking lot. I looked around too. (One thing you should know about me: I'm curious. Way too curious, some folks would say.)

That's when I spotted him, lingering behind a parked car two rows away, like he was waiting for someone. A guy with shaggy, shoulder-length brown hair and a restless way of moving that raised my radar. (See, I've got this radar for trouble and it's almost never wrong.)

Hunched inside a shabby overcoat, hands jammed deep in his pockets, he was kind of scuzzy. The guy wore raggedy jeans and worn high-top sneakers. I had this weird feeling about him, like I'd seen him somewhere before. I stole a quick look at DeLyn, wondering if she'd been looking for him. But her eyes were flitting in another direction.

Ignore him, I told myself. You're here to watch George fence—don't let your detective imagination run away with you. I focused on the conversation.

"We'd better go inside now," George said. "Bela hates it when we're late. He says that discipline is the most important element of fencing."

DeLyn rolled her eyes. "Bela says a lot of things, George," she muttered.

"What was that?" George asked brightly.

"Nothing," DeLyn replied. "Let's go in."

We filed along with the spectators entering the

field house. Inside the cavernous space, bleachers were set up along all four walls. Over the field house floor, where I'd often played basketball, several long beige plastic mats had been rolled out lengthwise. Each was about fifteen yards long and six feet wide. Lots of wires and cables snaked across the floor, attached to clunky metal boxes.

"Is this where they fence?" Bess asked uncertainly.

"Sure, over there on those strips," Damon explained. "During a tournament, several bouts take place at the same time, each one on its own strip. It can get pretty confusing. But each bout has its own referee, and those electronic boxes keep score. You'll see when they get started. The black screen on the side of the box lights up and shows the score."

"Damon, look, the TV station sent a news reporter," DeLyn said, tugging on her brother's sleeve and pointing.

We looked over to the end of the field house, where the basketball hoops were normally hung. A cameraman was assembling his equipment, while a petite woman in a pink sweater and black pants was testing out a recording mike.

For some reason, Damon didn't look exactly happy about this new development. "Since when does the local station care about fencing?" he grumbled. "There must be some mistake—they must have thought they were coming here to cover a basketball game."

"Now, Damon, you've heard what Bela says," George reminded him. "Thanks to all the great competition in the area, the local fencing scene is getting hot."

"It's certainly more interesting than the usual local news," Ned said. "I mean, who wants to watch another grocery store grand opening?"

"Maybe Bela called the station himself and told them about the tournament," George said. "It'll be free publicity for the salle."

"Ooh, George, your first victory might be captured on TV," Bess exclaimed. "But how do we know which space you'll be fencing on?"

Damon shrugged, still looking uneasily at the camera crew. "Bela will tell us who's fencing where and when, and we'll tell you so you can be in the right place. Each fencer has several bouts scheduled against different opponents. It depends on how many fencers are registered for each class. We're all ranked according to age and experience."

George smiled. "Yeah, good thing. A novice like me won't have to face old pros like DeLyn and Damon."

I checked out DeLyn's response—a lukewarm smile and averted eyes. What was her problem? She and George were supposed to be friends. I didn't get why she was acting so cold.

"There are different events for different weapons, too," Damon went on. "Foil—that's what George is fencing with now. And then épée and saber."

"Those are larger swords," George explained.

"And heavier. Plus, they're covered by different rules," Damon added. "With épée and saber, you see . . ."

My mind drifted back to the scuzzy guy in the parking lot. I finally remembered where I'd seen him before. It was last Saturday, outside Bela Kovacs's fencing studio. I'd been there picking up George after her lesson. He was sitting on a bench and minding his own business, but something about him told me he was up to no good.

"This is no time to lose your focus!" a man's voice snapped beside me. I jumped slightly, pulled back from my wandering thoughts.

A wiry man in a neatly pressed suit and tie had joined our group. His longish hair stuck out in all directions, dark and curly with streaks of silver at the temples. His eyes were dark and fiery, too, with shadowy circles underneath. The Brittany twins' great posture was nothing compared to this guy's. He stood completely lithe and erect. Something about him crackled with energy.

Behind him I caught sight of Ned's face, flickering with panic. I've hardly ever seen Ned scared of anything, so it was a total shock. Stranger still, a split second later he melted into the crowd and vanished.

"Bela!" George greeted the man eagerly.

In one move, Bela managed to scowl at DeLyn, toss Damon a look of scorn, and then pivot tenderly toward George. "My precious prodigy!" he exclaimed, rolling his r's with a European accent. "I trust you slept well last night and had a robust breakfast? Preparation is paramount!"

Believe it or not, George—my buddy George—actually blushed at her fencing master's words. "I know, Bela," she said meekly.

"You, my child, my great new discovery," Kovacs declared with a flourish of his left hand. "You will make me proud today, yes?"

George grinned. "I'll try my best."

Kovacs took hold of George's shoulders and, bending forward, planted a good-luck kiss on her forehead. "Your best, and nothing less," he murmured proudly. "Then victory is assured." He dropped his hands and swiveled toward DeLyn. "And what have you to say for yourself?" he barked.

DeLyn clenched her jaw. "I'm ready, Bela."

"Are you?" Kovacs cocked a shaggy eyebrow, and his nostrils flared. "I haven't seen you do your stretching exercises yet. You've drawn Una for your first bout, you know. *Una.*" His lip curled in scorn.

9

"You're kidding—Una?" Damon asked with a nervous twitch.

DeLyn shrugged carelessly. "No big deal, Bela—I've beaten her before."

"Have you? Have you beaten her *lately*?" Kovacs scoffed. His dark eyes drilled into hers for a moment. Then he spun on his heel and stalked away.

DeLyn Brittany stared after him with such hurt and despair, it almost broke my heart.

The Rivals

Right then and there, I took back everything negative I had thought about DeLyn Brittany. No wonder she was acting weird around George—she was jealous! George had evidently become the fencing master's new star, and DeLyn felt threatened. That was only natural.

"Who's this Una you're all talking about?" Bess asked Damon.

Damon took his eyes off his sister's stricken face. "Una Merrick. She fences for Salle Olympique, over in Cutler Falls."

"Salle Olympique?" George repeated. "Our big rival?"

DeLyn tossed her head. "They think they're our rivals. But Salle Budapest is better than Salle

11

Olympique. We'll show them this afternoon."

"That's right," Damon said, clenching his fist. "Lyndie, you can beat that spoiled rich girl. Teach Una who's boss. I'll be rooting for you. Come on, let's start our warm-up stretches."

As the Brittany twins slipped off through the crowd, I turned to George for information. "I know Kovacs's studio is called Salle Budapest. But Salle Olympique?"

"The word *salle* is French for 'room.' In fencing, it's the technical term for any fencing school," George explained. "Bela named his Salle Budapest because he's Hungarian, from Budapest. There's a great tradition of fencing in Hungary. Salle Olympique is run by a Frenchman named Paul Mourbiers. I've seen him around. He should be—oh yeah, there he is."

She pointed across the tournament floor. I followed her finger and saw a tall, slim man with dark red hair, cut short and severe. Even though he was Bela Kovacs's physical opposite, the similarities between the two were striking. Both wore dark suits and had elegant postures, and they gave off the same vibrant energy. They're like clones, I thought to myself. I bet that Paul Mourbiers had the same manners—or lack of them—that Bela Kovacs did.

Mourbiers began to cross the field house floor

with long, precise strides, swerving around the fencing strips. Next to me, George drew in a sharp breath. Then—was it my imagination?—a nervous hush seemed to settle over the field house, as if several people were holding their breath all at once.

It didn't take more than a second for me to spot what others had already seen. Bela Kovacs, wild hair flying, was walking purposefully across the fencing floor from the other side. Though neither of them appeared to notice the other, the two fencing masters were definitely on course to collide.

Which one would step aside first?

"Go, Bela," I heard George mutter softly beside me.

They were within a few feet of each other now. Mourbiers's chin was lifted high and his hands were clasped behind his back. He refused to look at Kovacs. Meanwhile, Kovacs's jaw was set like a bulldog's, his eyes were studiously on the ground, and his hands were planted stubbornly behind his back. Each man refused to look the other's way.

And then, as if on cue, both teachers swung their eyes to the center. Their gazes met and locked. Even from yards away, I felt the heat of their smoldering glares. Decades of hatred seemed poured into that one instant of eye contact.

People all around me gasped.

And then Kovacs and Mourbiers walked past each other—Mourbiers with a disdainful shrug, Kovacs with a defiant head toss. That was it. Moment over.

"Wow, what was that about?" I whispered to George, as the room began to buzz again with conversation.

"Don't even ask," George groaned. "Bela hates Paul Mourbiers—hates him with a passion. Mourbiers moved into the area and started his fencing salle six years ago. He really cut into Bela's business. But the whole thing between them goes back a lot further. I'll explain later—right now I have to go warm up. The preparation routine is essential, Bela says."

"Sure thing. Good luck, George!" I said as she walked away.

"Break a leg!" Bess added.

"I don't think you're supposed to say that," I reminded Bess. "That's only for actors in a play. We don't really want George to break a leg here."

"Whatever," Bess said with a giggle and a shake of her hair. "It sure looks like theater to me."

"Our first bouts are about to begin. Will spectators please leave the fencing floor," a voice announced over the PA system. Bess and I headed for the bleachers. We'd forgotten to ask which fencing strips George, DeLyn, and Damon would be competing on, but the stands weren't crowded—I figured we could move to the best viewing spot when we saw our friends arrive on their strips.

Looking up into the bleachers, I spotted Ned. He gave me a sheepish wave. I shook my head as I hopped up the steps to join him. "You are such a coward," I teased him. "The minute you saw Bela Kovacs, you ran for the hills."

"What can I say? The man scares me," Ned admitted. "I got this awful feeling in my stomach as soon as I saw him. I had to disappear."

"Hi, Nancy," said Evaline Waters, who was sitting right next to Ned.

"Evaline! It's so great to see you," I replied.

Before she retired, Evaline Waters was the head librarian at the local public library. I've known her for years, but apparently I didn't know her that well. "I didn't know you were a fencing fan," I said.

"Oh, I've always loved fencing," Evaline declared. "Never tried it myself, but I do love to watch it. When I was a girl, one of my favorite books was *The Three Musketeers*—you know, the French classic by Alexandre Dumas."

"I saw that movie!" Bess chipped in. "It had a ton of cute actors in it."

Evaline smiled. "Yes, it did, Bess. But the movie isn't nearly as good as the book. It tells you everything you'd want to know about the old traditions of chivalry. The musketeers weren't just swashbuckling swordsmen, you know. They lived and died by a code of honor. They were noble figures in an age of deadly rivalries and rampant corruption." Leaning closer, Evaline whispered ominously, "Not so different from the present day, I might add."

"I'm with you on that, Evaline—*The Three Musketeers* is a great book," Ned said. Ned is as much of a book lover as Evaline is. He's majoring in English in college. "But there's no way Bess is going to read it— not if her alternative is watching a movie with lots of cute actors."

Bess made a face and pretended to punch Ned in the arm.

Ned can't resist teasing Bess every once in a while—he's like a brother to her, and George, too. He's a little bit more than a brother to me, though. Don't get me wrong, I'm not one of those girls who's always checking out cute guys. I'm too busy doing my own thing. But Ned's special. We've been going out ever since junior high. Over the years, we've learned to give each other space, which is something I need. Of course, every now and then, Ned will give me one of those swoony looks with his big brown eyes, and then I remember how great it is to have him around.

I scanned the fencing floor and saw DeLyn standing beside a fencing strip, zipping up her high-necked white jacket. A referee beside her was fiddling with a long electrical cord and a vest made of silver fabric. He attached the cord to the silver vest and handed it to DeLyn. She slipped it on over her jacket.

"That vest is called a lamé," Evaline explained. "It's got metal threads woven into the fabric, to pick up electrical impulses. Every time a fencer is touched by his opponent's sword, it sends a signal to the scoring box."

"Seems fair," I said. "No one can argue whether or not the sword made contact if it's been measured electronically."

"If only it were that simple," Evaline said with a smile. "As you'll see, there are still plenty of disputes. The referee rules whether sword contact deserves to score a point, and there are many reasons why a touch might be disqualified. It could land on the wrong part of the body, for example. In a foil bout, you can only hit your opponent on the torso. A larger body area is allowed for saber fencers, and even more for épée fencers."

"So that's why fencers specialize in one weapon—each involves a different fighting strategy," Ned said.

"You've got it," Evaline said. "Most fencers start out with the foil, the lightest and most flexible sword. But once they get into fencing, they may choose to concentrate on another weapon. For instance, that African-American girl down there, DeLyn Brittany——"

"Oh, we know DeLyn. She's a friend of George's," I told Evaline.

"Really?" Evaline said. "She's very good. It looks like she's fighting with a foil right now, and sometimes she fences saber, but usually she fences épée. Now, her brother——"

"Yeah, Damon. We met him, too," Bess said.

Evaline nodded. "Damon specializes in saber, which is the heaviest sword of all. Generally, only men compete in saber. We should see his match later on."

Bess frowned and pointed toward DeLyn and the referee. "Look, he's checking out her sword. Is there something wrong? Is he going to disqualify her?"

"That's standard procedure," Evaline replied. "The referee checks each fencer's equipment and clothing before a match, to make sure nobody gets hurt."

"Makes sense," Ned said. "They are going at each other with deadly weapons, after all."

"It's not like it's dangerous," said Bess. "George showed me her sword—it's got a protective tip on it."

Ned gave her a skeptical look. "Believe me, when someone comes at you with a slashing sword, you

18

could still get hurt. The side edges of the blade are sharp, not rounded. And okay, maybe they're not razor sharp, but they can still scratch you. Plus, that sword is made of tough metal. It can definitely bruise."

"That's why fencers wear padded protective clothing," Evaline said.

"As well as a mask of metal mesh that covers the entire face," I added.

"Those masks are a pain to wear," Ned said with a groan. "They're heavy, and if you don't fasten the straps well, they rattle around, and they can cut off your side vision. Plus, you get really hot underneath."

I had to smile. "Sounds like you really loved fencing, huh?" I asked.

"Oh, yeah," Ned replied, equally sarcastic.

The referee now stepped over to inspect DeLyn's opponent, a tall girl with short-cropped strawberry blond hair. She had arrived late and was still zipping up her jacket. She looked like a sorority girl, the type who didn't want to mess up her sleek haircut or her carefully applied makeup. The referee pointed at his watch and gestured impatiently for her to hurry up.

"So that's the famous Una," Bess commented. "She has very long arms and legs, doesn't she?"

"That's a great advantage," Evaline said. "If your arms are longer than your opponent's, you can touch her with your sword from a distance where she can't reach you. But DeLyn has other advantages—speed, for one thing. I've seen these two girls fence before, both in local tournaments and in college matches. DeLyn and her brother started this year on the University of River Heights team. Una's been fencing for Moreton College for a couple of years."

Bouts had begun on other fencing strips around the field house. Hurrying things along, DeLyn's referee gave Una a hasty pat on her shoulder. He grabbed the electronic cord attached to her lamé and followed it over to a heavy domed base, about two feet across, on the floor at the far end of the strip. He checked that the cord was firmly attached to the base, as he had already done with DeLyn's body cord. Then he waved to the two fencers to take their places.

Each girl stood behind a line on her end of the long strip, about a third of the way from the midpoint. They touched their sword hilts respectfully to the front of their masks and bowed slightly toward the referee, who bowed back. Then they pivoted and bowed toward the nearest spectators. Finally, they faced each other and bowed a third time.

"That's so nice!" Bess exclaimed. "Even before they start fighting, they make friends."

Evaline chuckled. "They're required to do that, Bess," she explained. "If they forget, they could be disqualified. It's just part of the fencing ritual."

Bess shrugged. "It still seems nice," she said.

Having finished their salutes, the two fencers struck "ready" poses: faces front, shoulders angled sideways, legs flexed in a crouch, swords pointing to the ceiling, free hand crooked at shoulder height behind them.

"It's almost like a dance, isn't it?" Bess remarked.

"En garde," the referee called out. The two girls lowered their foils, pointing them directly at each other's hearts.

"Are you ready?" the referee asked. Both girls nodded. "Fence!" he commanded.

I had to admire DeLyn's aggressive fencing style. With fierce determination, she lunged forward on the fencing strip. Una scuttled backward, swinging her foil diagonally to fend off DeLyn's thrusts. Metal clanged on metal, and light flashed off the dancing blades.

An electrical beep signaled the bout's first touch. "Halt!" the referee called. Both girls stopped, straightened up, raised their foils, and returned to their starting lines. A yellow light on the scoring box indicated DeLyn's side of the strip. "Oh, good, DeLyn scored the first point," Evaline said.

"How many points do you need to win?" I asked.

"In this tournament, it's whoever scores five

touches first," Evaline said. "Every fencer today meets every other fencer in his or her age class and keeps an overall tally. If this were a direct elimination bout, though, it would take fifteen touches to win. The loser would then be out of the tournament for good."

The referee called *"En garde"* again and the girls crouched into their ready positions. Soon they were lunging up and down the strip once more.

"What if you step off the strip?" Bess asked.

"Then you're disqualified," Evaline said. "You can also be disqualified if you touch your sword point to the floor, or if you turn your back on your opponent."

"Whoa, you have to remember all that?" Bess asked. "While somebody is running toward you with a sword? I'd be so nervous, I'd forget."

"You know what would make me nervous? Bela Kovacs watching my every move," Ned said. He nodded toward the fencing floor. The Hungarian fencing master was pacing up and down near DeLyn's strip. And on the other side, Paul Mourbiers was doing exactly the same thing, focusing on Una.

Now that Ned had pointed them out, I couldn't take my eyes off the two coaches. Their body language was as fascinating as the bout itself. When Una scored the next touch, Mourbiers pumped a fist and clapped his hands. He stole a triumphant glance at Kovacs, who ran his hands angrily through his wild mop of hair. But a moment later, when the referee called out "Illegal touch," Kovacs was the one cheering.

"What just happened?" asked Bess.

"She touched DeLyn's shoulder, not her torso," Evaline explained. "So this time, they start fencing again from wherever they were when the signal beeped. That gives DeLyn an advantage—she's already forced Una pretty far back on the strip."

The referee called out "Fence!" and the girls' swords began to fly again. Their soft-soled shoes set up a rhythm on the plastic surface—shuffle, shuffle, pound, *clash!* as one girl pressed forward and then lunged for the attack. Then it was shuffle, shuffle, pound, *clash!* as the other girl responded.

DeLyn and Una moved up and down the strip, advancing and retreating. Kovacs and Mourbiers strode in tandem alongside them, gesticulating wildly. It was almost as if the fencers were their puppets. "Attack, attack," Kovacs barked at DeLyn.

"Why is Mourbiers shouting to Una about Paris?" Bess asked.

Evaline suppressed a grin. "It does sound like he's saying 'Paris,' with a French accent—*Par-ee*," she agreed. "But he's telling her to *parry*—p-a-r-r-y. It's a technical term for a defensive move, where you swing your sword crosswise to block your opponent's strike—"

Just then Una dropped her foil. I heard the tinny clatter as it bounced off the mat and onto the bare hardwood floor. Everyone around us gasped and jumped to their feet. I jumped up too, trying to see over their heads.

Una was kneeling on the mat, moaning and clutching her right wrist.

And there, on her sleeve, a spot of bright red was growing, staining her clean white doublet.

Blood.

3

The Gauntlet Is Down

The referee, Mourbiers, and Kovacs closed in around Una. DeLyn stood alone on the fencing strip, still holding her sword. As she pushed her mask up onto the top of her head, her face looked creased with concern.

An assistant came running over with a first-aid kit. "What's going to happen now?" I asked Evaline anxiously.

"If it's just a minor injury, they'll patch her up quickly and go on with the bout. They can suspend it for as long as ten minutes," she explained. "Of course, if the injury's more serious, they'll stop the bout. Una would have to forfeit."

I glanced at DeLyn standing awkwardly on the strip, with her sword tucked under her arm. I could guess how she felt. Even though she hadn't planned to hurt Una, she felt responsible. If Una forfeited, it wouldn't seem like much of a victory.

Bela Kovacs stood up and walked away. I was surprised that he didn't go over to reassure DeLyn. I just assumed that after making sure Una wasn't badly hurt, his first priority would be to support his athlete.

A moment later Paul Mourbiers stood too. In one hand he clutched the long, padded white glove Una had been wearing on her sword hand. I could see a bright smear of blood on its deep, flared cuff. He waved it in Kovacs's face.

"Now what is Paul doing with that gauntlet? What are those two buffoons up to?" Evaline murmured.

"You know about their rivalry?" I asked her.

"Dear me, everybody in town knows about their rivalry—or at least, everybody who follows fencing does." Evaline clucked her tongue. "Every tournament, Paul and Bela find some excuse for an argument. No matter whether it's a federation tournament, or a practice meet like this one, or a college match-up, Bela and Paul are involved in every fencing event in the area."

I watched the two men yell at each other, red faced, with their hands waving. "I can understand why Mourbiers would be upset that his fencer got injured," I said. "But why should he act like it's the other coach's fault?"

"Mourbiers blames Kovacs whenever he can," Evaline said. "And Kovacs does the same."

"George said when Mourbiers opened his salle a few years ago, it really hurt Kovacs's business," Bess added.

"It wasn't just a question of business," Evaline said. "With these men, it's personal. Bela has a terrible temper. Often he's the one who loses his head when they argue. But in my opinion, Mourbiers deliberately provokes him. He plays that guy like a violin! Why, from the very first day, when Mourbiers opened his salle, he had the nerve to name it Salle Olympique. No wonder Kovacs can't stand him."

Ned looked baffled. "Because it sounds like he's training Olympic-quality fencers, and Kovacs isn't?"

Evaline shook her head. "It's more than that. Apparently everything between them stems back to the 1976 Olympics in Montreal. They fenced against each other there. I never heard who won. But it seems there was some kind of disagreement. Decades later, they still haven't gotten over it." She chuckled. "That must be why the TV newspeople came today. They've heard about the crazy feud between those two. Well, their hunch seems to have paid off." She nodded toward the TV crew, filming away at the edge

27

of the fencing floor. "They're bound to get some good footage out of this."

I don't know why, but my gut instinct told me there was more going on here than an ancient personal grudge. I couldn't see Una, so I didn't know how serious her injury was. But I could see the anxious look on DeLyn's face. Something told me it was time to get more information.

"Nancy, where are you going?" Bess asked as I climbed down the bleachers.

"I just need to check something out," I said. "I'll be right back."

In a moment I was in the thick of the crowd milling around the fencing strip. Other bouts were still in progress, but the attention of the field house was focused on DeLyn's fencing strip. Since I'd never been to a fencing match before, I didn't know if injuries like this were common. Even if they were, though, I had a feeling that people were watching this bout in hopes of a fight between Kovacs and Mourbiers.

As I worked my way deeper into the crowd, I started to feel the back of my neck prickle. Sensing that something was up, I stopped and searched the crowd around me.

Out of the corner of my eye, I spied a familiar figure—a troubling figure. I spun around and spotted the shapeless brown overcoat, the ratty sneakers, and the stringy dark hair. What was that raggedy guy from the parking lot doing here? And why was he so agitated? His eyes looked dilated with fear, and he bit his lower lip so intently I was afraid he'd soon bleed. Clenching his fists at his sides, rocking from foot to foot, he was like a time bomb ready to go off.

I took a step toward him—and he saw me. His eyes widened and he recoiled, ducking behind the large woman next to him.

Suddenly somebody bumped into me from the other side. Someone else stepped on my foot. And by the time I'd gotten away from the crowd, he'd vanished.

Disappointed, I turned back toward the knot of people surrounding Una. I was close enough now to see the doctor—or at least a man with a medical bag—kneeling beside Una, wrapping white gauze around her forearm. "The gash is long, but it's not too deep," I heard him say. "No need for stitches, but you'd better keep it well bandaged."

I edged closer, ears straining.

"Somehow, the seam on her gauntlet came loose," the referee said to the doctor. "Her bare arm was exposed to the foil." He twisted around, looking over his shoulder. "Where is that gauntlet? Paul, do you still have it?"

Paul Mourbiers hustled forward, saying, "Here is

the gauntlet, Gary. I'm not sure it belongs to Una, though. It doesn't have her name written on it. Una always labels all her equipment with her name. I teach this procedure to all students at my salle."

The referee took the glove from Mourbiers. He fingered the broken stitching along the side, where the suede palm was attached to the padded cotton of the back and cuff. My fingers itched to get hold of the glove so I could inspect it myself, but I had no official reason to do that. Still, I sidled up closer to the referee. If he happened to lay it down and I happened to pick it up . . .

"This could have broken open during the bout," the referee mused, staring at the glove. "Those girls were fencing quite vigorously. Stitches do break in the heat of fighting."

Mourbiers tilted his head, looked down his nose, and raised one eyebrow. "You were under pressure to begin the bout on time, Gary—are you sure you inspected all the equipment beforehand?"

The referee pressed his lips together in an exasperated expression. I guessed he'd dealt with Mourbiers and Kovacs before. "What are you saying, Paul?"

Mourbiers's dark eyes glittered with suspicion. "Perhaps *someone* substituted this faulty gauntlet, knowing it would split open—and my girl would be hurt."

The referee stood up, slapping the gauntlet against

his palm. "If you want to lodge a formal complaint, Mourbiers, go ahead. Otherwise, we're running out of time. The ten-minute time limit is almost up. You'll have to make a decision. Does your fencer feel ready to continue the bout, or do you want to forfeit?"

Mourbiers's upper lip twitched slightly, but he restrained himself. He turned to Una, lightly tapping her hand inside the gauze swaddling.

"What do you say, Una?" he asked. "Can you carry on? It would be a shame to forfeit." He slid a quick glare toward Bela Kovacs.

On the other side of the fencing strip, Kovacs stood with his shoulders hunched high, chin tucked down, and eyes spitting with fury. "Do you intend to file a complaint now?" Kovacs snarled. "Is this the Salle Olympique strategy—to go whining to the authorities whenever a match goes against you?"

Facing him across the mat, Paul Mourbiers was like his mirror image—same clenched fists, same tense neck muscles, same glowering eyes. Sure they were mad at each other before, but now they looked like they were about to explode.

Una climbed to her feet, lifting her bandaged arm gingerly. "It's better now, Paul, I think I can fence after all . . . ," she said. She didn't look too certain to me, but I sensed she'd do anything to break the standoff between the two coaches.

But they scarcely heard her. "What else do you expect us to do?" Mourbiers growled across the mat at his rival. "Rigging the bout—that's standard operating procedure for you, isn't it?"

Kovacs's voice came out half-strangled with rage. "Rigging the bout? Why would I even need to do such a thing? My fencer could beat yours with one hand tied behind her back!"

The referee spun around. "Bela!" he said in a warning voice.

"You accuse me of cheating? Look at your own cheating!" Kovacs sputtered at Mourbiers.

"That's it!" the ref said firmly. "Yellow card on Salle Budapest! Unsportsmanlike behavior."

Everyone nearby froze. I could hear DeLyn gasp behind me.

"If you want, we can start fencing again," Una's voice piped up shyly.

"Yes, please, we want to finish our bout," DeLyn protested.

It was like Bela Kovacs had gone deaf from rage. He didn't respond to the fencers' offer. Nor did he react to the official's ruling. His eyes bore intensely into those of his rival. "The only skill you possess to teach your students is the fine art of cheating! You are truly a master at that," Kovacs yelled. "You've polished those skills for decades. Liar! Cheater!"

"Bela, you've already been given a warning card," the referee said. "Watch your language."

And that's when Kovacs really lost it. I can't tell you exactly what he said—he used words I'd never repeat. So let's just say I've never seen or heard an adult flip out like that.

A second official came running over from another bout. He grabbed Kovacs's shoulder. DeLyn ran to her coach, pleading, "Bela, please, calm down!" But the fencing master kept on shouting obscenities.

Somewhere in the middle of it, the referee called out, "Red card on Salle Budapest! Disqualification! Forfeit!"

"Forfeit?" DeLyn cried out, spinning to face the ref. "But we wanted to restart the bout. Can't you just let us fence again? I was ahead in the scoring!"

Bela Kovacs tore out of the official's grasp and hurtled toward Paul Mourbiers. "I'll get you for this!" he roared.

Kovacs lowered his head like a bull and plowed straight into Mourbiers's stomach. "Oof!" said Mourbiers, as he bent over and collapsed on the gym floor.

I was shoved aside as the TV cameraman pushed forward, trampling my foot. After struggling to get a better view, I saw the fencing teachers, rolling on the fencing mat like a couple of eight-year-olds. Kovacs and Mourbiers were a tangle of swinging fists, jabbing elbows, and crunching knees. And the cameraman was getting it all on film.

Mourbiers had his arms over his head, cringing under the Hungarian's blows. But then, for just a second, I got a look at Mourbiers's face.

And I could swear he was wearing a grin of triumph.

4

Bad News

My thoughts flashed back to what Evaline Waters had said: "Bela may be the one who loses his temper, but Mourbiers deliberately provokes him." That cunning grin of his aroused my suspicions. Could Mourbiers have planned this fistfight all along?

And if so, why?

Two fencing officials stepped in to pull the coaches off each other. Other officials began to shoo spectators off the fencing floor. The TV cameraman was asked to turn off his camera and harsh lights. Kovacs and Mourbiers were led away to a side area where they could sort out their dispute verbally.

Since I couldn't follow them without being completely conspicuous, I rejoined my friends. "Wow,

Nancy, did you see them punching each other?" Bess asked.

I nodded. "Yup. At least, Kovacs was punching Mourbiers. It didn't look to me like Mourbiers was hitting back much."

"It all got out of hand so quickly," Ned said.

I stole another glance at Paul Mourbiers, who was dusting off his suit and smoothing back his short auburn hair. He didn't look too upset. Bela Kovacs was another matter. His hair stuck out in all directions, his eyes were flashing, and his tie was askew. His once-crisp dress shirt gaped open where buttons had popped off during the fight. "Evaline, what was it you said earlier—about Paul Mourbiers provoking Bela Kovacs on purpose?" I asked.

My friend the librarian gave me a shrewd look. "I've said it before and I'll say it again: Paul Mourbiers plays that guy like a violin!"

I was surprised—usually Evaline isn't so cynical about people.

"Bess," I said slowly, "remember before the match, we were wondering why the TV crew came to this event."

"Yes," Bess said. "And George suggested that Bela Kovacs told them about it, to drum up publicity for Salle Budapest."

Ned shook his head. "Boy, if he did, it backfired on

him. This news coverage will be terrible for his salle's reputation."

"I agree," I said. "But we have no evidence Bela Kovacs called the TV station. Only, I was just thinking—who else might have made such a call?"

Evaline raised her eyebrows. "Paul Mourbiers. He also has a vested interest in attracting publicity for fencing, doesn't he?"

"Exactly," I said. "In fact, the way things developed, it couldn't have worked out better for Salle Olympique."

"Or worse for Salle Budapest," Ned finished my thought. "But do you really think Mourbiers would go that far, just to smear a rival?"

I looked over at Evaline. "Ms. Waters, you've followed their feud for some time. What do you think?"

The librarian looked troubled. "My goodness, Nancy, I'd hate to think anyone would stoop that low."

I looked at the fencing floor. Things seemed to have settled down. Fresh bouts were taking place on all the fencing strips. I spotted Kovacs, huddled now at the far end of the field house with George and Damon, but there was no sign of DeLyn. Not that I blamed her. Kovacs's rotten temper had cost her a victory.

Una sat on her equipment bag, cradling her bandaged arm in her lap, just a few yards away.

Her coach was on the other side of the fencing

floor, talking into the TV reporter's microphone—smiling and nodding, being very French and very charming.

I got that uneasy feeling in the pit of my stomach, the one I get when I sense someone's not playing fair. Had Paul Mourbiers convinced the television station to cover this tournament, knowing all along that he would goad Bela Kovacs into an ugly public fight?

And if so, how far had he gone to make Bela Kovacs look bad?

Had he given his own fencer a damaged gauntlet, knowing that she might get hurt—just for the sake of a little publicity?

Back at home that night, I huddled in an armchair reading, while Hannah did needlepoint and my dad read the paper. The television hummed quietly in the background.

"Why, look, Nancy," said Hannah. "They're talking about that fencing tournament you went to today."

I looked up from my book, suddenly alert. "Oh, no. Turn up the sound, Dad."

My dad lowered his newspaper and tapped the volume button on the remote control. "That's right, George is a fencer now. How did she do in her first meet?"

"George? Oh, she lost," I said, distracted. "Shhh."

The petite reporter in the pink sweater was on the screen. "We all know about the noble art of fencing," she began. "What started out as two guys with swords trying to kill each other has been tamed over the centuries into a beautiful sport, with traditions, rules, and courtly ceremony." The image on the screen showed two fencers I didn't recognize, touching their swords to their masks and bowing to each other before their bout.

The reporter paused for a beat. "Or has it?"

The camera image switched to a close-up of Bela Kovacs and Paul Mourbiers rolling on the floor, raining blows on each other.

"This was the scene today at a 'friendly' fencing meet at the University of River Heights field house," the reporter said. "Two fencing coaches got into a heated dispute when an equipment malfunction led to an injury for one young woman fencer. Officials penalized Bela Kovacs, of Salle Budapest in River Heights, for 'going to the mat' with his colleague Paul Mourbiers, of Salle Olympique in Cutler Falls."

The camera cut to Mourbiers, being interviewed after the fight. "It is very unfortunate when an adult behaves in such a childish fashion," he said, pursing his lips and playing up his French accent. "A man who should be a role model for his students—it's a shame. The officials were correct to disqualify him."

The reporter asked, "What was the equipment malfunction?"

Mourbiers held up Una's torn gauntlet. "This glove—we call it a gauntlet—is supposed to protect the sword hand of the fencer during a match," he explained. "My protégée, Una Merrick—a lovely young girl and a marvelous fencing talent—suffered a bloody gash all up her arm because this gauntlet split open."

There was a quick cut to Una, holding up her bandaged arm. From the miserable expression on her face, I could guess she wasn't happy about showing off her injury on TV.

The camera went back to Mourbiers. "When the referee looked at the glove," he continued, "it became clear that it was not Una's own glove. Someone must have placed this damaged gauntlet with her equipment. I merely questioned the referee about the possibility of sabotage, and then suddenly this other coach, this Kovacs fellow—that's Bela Kovacs, who runs the Salle Budapest fencing school—got completely out of hand." The image on screen switched to footage of Kovacs charging at Mourbiers, his hair wild and his eyes blazing.

"Do you think this penalty has taught him a lesson?" the reporter asked.

Mourbiers shrugged expressively and cast a sorrowful look up to the ceiling. "If only life were that simple. But I don't know if it is possible for an old dog like Bela Kovacs to learn such new tricks. He learned the sport many years ago in Hungary, you see. Hungarians were always known to be vicious fighters. Like Attila the Hun, for example."

My father snorted. "That's a low blow, bringing in Attila the Hun!"

"Bela Kovacs carries on that tradition of winning at all costs," Mourbiers continued. "I've known Bela many years. We met when we competed against each other in '76, at the Olympics in Montreal. There were rumors about him even then. I don't know—if I were hiring a fencing master to teach my child this sport, I wouldn't send him to study with a man of such questionable reputation. I wouldn't send him to Salle Budapest."

The reporter faced the camera and announced, "This is Kelly Chaffetz, at the University of River Heights field house. Steve, back to you."

My dad lowered the volume as the next segment began—late-breaking coverage of a grocery store grand opening over in Farmingville. "That must have been some fencing match," he said. "Did you witness the fight, Nan?"

I sighed. "Yes, I was right there. One of George's friends was involved."

"The girl with the bandaged arm?" Hannah asked, her voice full of concern.

I shook my head. "No, George's friend DeLyn caused the injury. She didn't mean to—in fact, she felt pretty lousy about hurting her opponent. And on top of that, she lost the bout because her coach started the fight."

"So her coach is this Hungarian man?" Dad clarified. His lips twitched with a smile he couldn't ward off. "Attila the Hun's descendant?"

"Come on, Dad, Bela Kovacs isn't that bad," I protested.

"Of course he isn't!" Dad said. "It was so obvious that Frenchman was trying to ruin his competitor's reputation. I'm just surprised the TV station ran such a one-sided piece. But you, Nancy, I trust. So what's your impression of Bela Kovacs?"

I settled back in my chair, trying to sort out my thoughts. "Well, he's not a guy I'd invite to dinner anytime soon," I admitted. "He isn't the model of a supportive, nurturing teacher. Ned took a couple of classes with him last winter and he's terrified of him."

Hannah paused in her needlework. "Ned? Why, that boy usually gets along very well with people." Hannah's kind of partial to Ned Nickerson, for obvious reasons.

"But on the other hand, George takes fencing lessons from Bela Kovacs and she thinks the world of him," I said, determined to be fair-minded.

"I don't need hearsay. I need your direct impression," my father insisted. He's a lawyer—and a pretty successful one at that. He hates fuzzy thinking. I guess I get that from him too.

I thought for a minute. "I did see Kovacs speak pretty rudely to George's friend DeLyn, and it made me uncomfortable. But he was giving her solid coaching advice, about doing warm-ups and preparing mentally for her match. I never heard him tell her to cheat."

Dad nodded. "In the law, we have some pretty clear guidelines about this sort of thing," he said. "You can be sued if you spread lies about someone. Even if the information you spread is true, you can still be sued for slander if it's proven you did it for a malicious reason. Now, clearly this Mourbiers fellow is trying to ruin Bela Kovacs's reputation. For all we know, those accusations may be true. But he has no right to go on television and make such remarks, especially not when Kovacs had no chance to defend himself."

"That poor man's business could be ruined by this," Hannah said, jabbing her needle into her canvas with an outraged scowl.

"Are you saying Bela Kovacs could sue Paul Mourbiers for slander, Dad?" I asked.

Dad tapped his temple, thinking. "I'm not sure he'd have a case," he said. "Those are usually tough cases to prove. First, he'd have to produce evidence that the news report cost him a significant amount of business. It's no good just saying someone made you look bad—you have to show concrete damages. And then you'd have to prove that Mourbiers did it intentionally."

"Like, for example, if Mourbiers had called the TV station and got them to cover the fencing tournament in the first place?"

Dad raised his eyebrows and asked, "Did he?"

"Maybe. It's just a hunch."

Dad rolled his eyes and lifted up his newspaper. "Hunches don't stand up in a court of law, Nancy. I hope you don't think this is another case for you to solve."

"No one has asked me to get involved," I answered. That was true—no one had. But I *was* starting to get curious on my own behalf.

"It sounds as if these two coaches go back a long way," Dad continued. "Whatever lies between them, you won't clear it up with a few discreet inquiries. You can't fix all the problems in the world, you know."

True. But when I thought about how miserable Una and DeLyn had looked when their coaches started fighting, it made me wish there was something I could do about it.

The next afternoon I parked outside Salle Budapest. I'd promised to pick up George after her fencing clinic, but I was also there because I was curious. I wondered whether Hannah was right. Could a small story on the nightly local news really destroy the reputation of Bela Kovacs?

I studied my surroundings for a minute before getting out of my car. I'd been to Salle Budapest several times before, meeting George before or after classes, but I'd never really looked at it before. It was a stand-alone, one-story cinder-block building, faced with tan bricks. It had a blacktop parking area surrounded by weeds, a garbage bin out back, and an air-conditioning unit humming alongside it. Nothing special.

I'd never paid attention before, so I couldn't tell if today there were fewer cars parked there than usual. As I scanned the lot, though, I did remember seeing Raggedy Man there a few days ago. Funny thing—I kept forgetting about that guy when other things were on my mind. But for some reason, I couldn't ignore him entirely. I didn't know yet if he was a piece in this fencing-school puzzle, but if he was, he sure didn't fit right.

Leaving my car, I went through the front entrance, a swinging glass door with the name SALLE BUDAPEST painted in curly red and black letters. The small raised entry area was cluttered with metal folding chairs and bulky canvas equipment bags that students had dumped onto the floor. Beyond an iron railing, you went down one step into the main studio, a large fluorescent-lit room with a varnished blond wood floor. One side wall was lined with mirrors. Accordion-fold doors along the other side wall hid shelves loaded with equipment—swords, masks, doublets, lamés, boxes of tangled electric body cords, scoring equipment. Until the tournament yesterday, I hadn't even known—or cared—what most of it was used for. At the back of the studio, a gray upholstered partition sectioned off a few office cubicles. It wasn't a very complicated setup.

I stepped over several equipment bags and perched on one of the folding chairs. I supposed they'd been put there so parents could wait for their children, but I'd never seen any parents there. It wasn't a cozy place to hang out.

While I waited for George, I tried to estimate whether there were fewer students here than usual.

The studio didn't look crowded, but then it never had when I'd been there before.

Seeing me, George came leaping over to the railing. She pushed her wire-mesh mask up and grinned. Her brown eyes sparkled, and she looked totally pumped up. "I just wanted to do one more round against Edwina," she said. "It won't take more than five minutes. Can you wait?"

"Sure, I'm in no hurry. Go ahead." I smiled. It was good to see George eager to fence again. She'd seemed kind of down after she lost her match yesterday.

"Bela gave me some really great tips for what to work on," George said. "He says that sometimes you benefit more from a loss than from a victory. That girl I fenced yesterday? Bela deliberately matched me against her because she was so much better than me. That's the best way to learn, Bela says. I scored more points against her than he expected! He was really proud."

"Good for you, George!" I said.

George fiddled with the silver duct tape wrapped around the point of her sword. "I thought something was weird—the electric button came disconnected," she said. "The machine didn't register when I touched Edwina's lamé. Now I'll beat her for sure!" She smacked her mask back down, whirled around, and bounced off to where her partner waited on the fencing strip.

Since it looked like I'd be staying for a while, and I was getting thirsty, I went off in search of some water. I tiptoed down the length of the main studio, carefully hugging close to the equipment closet wall—no point in getting in the way of the fencers. They would be armed and dangerous!

I reached the far end, where I suspected there would be a bathroom. I poked my head around the partition. Damon was sitting in the first cubicle, schoolbooks spread open on a battered metal desk. He looked up, smiled, and parted his lips to say hello. But just then we both heard Bela Kovacs bark from the next cubicle, "Damon! Is the answering machine on?"

"Yes, Bela," Damon said, rolling his eyes at me.

"Good!" Bela replied gruffly. "Don't waste your time answering the phone anymore."

"But Bela, you hired me to answer the phone," Damon replied, looking confused. "That was supposed to be my job—"

"Today it is not your job!" Bela snapped, peering over the partition. "Why pick up the nasty thing? It'll just be some more cowardly students canceling their lessons. Or maybe it will be another smothering, weak-willed parent, whining that she has to withdraw her spoiled offspring from my classes."

Damon sighed. "Now, Bela, you can't blame people for reacting to that news show. It's only natural, until they learn the true story...."

The cubicle wall shook as Kovacs pounded it in fury. "That scheming French weasel provoked me!" he shouted. Everyone in the salle could hear him, of course. A sick silence fell over the entire studio.

"You know the whole thing was a setup," Kovacs ranted on "Mourbiers got *his own fencer* to fake an injury, just to ruin me. In all my years, I have never seen such unethical conduct!"

Damon jumped up. "Bela, please, quiet down. Everyone's listening."

A moment's seething silence followed. I sidled away, trying to look casual. I didn't want to intrude— but I sure wanted to hear Bela's reply.

Draping himself over the cubicle wall, Damon went on in a soft, pleading voice, "This will die off in a few months, Bela. Students will return. They won't go all the way to Cutler Falls to study with Mourbiers—why, that's twenty miles! They might do it a few times, but they'll get tired of the drive and they'll come back here. Don't worry, Bela—your business will survive in the long run."

Another heavy silence. Then the old Hungarian's voice, shaking, replied, "The long run? Damon, how long do you expect me to wait this out?"

Damon hesitated. "A few months, maybe—four or five."

"Four or five months!" Bela snorted. "Is that all? And how do you propose I keep this business running until then?" He paused, as if trying to steady his shaking voice. Then he went on, slowly and wearily, "I can't wait that long, Damon. You know I put all my savings into this new building—and then borrowed more. The place is mortgaged to the hilt. The rates are so high—" I heard him slam his fist into the desk. "The bankers are bleeding me dry!"

He paused again. Then he spoke so softly, I had to lean forward to catch his words. "Every month I earn just enough for that month's payments. There is no cushion anymore. And my creditors have grown tired of my excuses. If I fall short this month . . . they will close me down." He paused, then burst out with a strangled sob. "Salle Budapest will be no more!"

5

The Setup

I couldn't see Bela Kovacs at that moment—and I didn't want to. It was bad enough to have to look at Damon Brittany's face. His eyes had gone blank and his mouth sagged open. His shoulders and chest sank, as if he were caving in from the inside.

Figuring that Damon didn't want anybody to see his pain at that moment, I ducked into the bathroom and pulled its flimsy wooden door shut behind me.

When I came out a minute later, Damon was gone. His books had been swept off the desk, the desk chair was still rocking, and the back door to the salle was swinging. He sure got out of there in a hurry.

Well, I couldn't blame him. The news of Kovacs's impending bankruptcy obviously upset Damon. I was impressed that someone like Damon, who had been with Bela for years—who really knew him—cared this much about the crusty old guy. That told me one thing: There must be more good in Bela Kovacs than I had realized.

And right now, he needed a friend.

Sometimes I have more nerve than is good for me. This was one of those times. Without a second thought, I walked around the wall of the inner cubicle and faced Bela Kovacs.

The Hungarian was slumped over his desk, head burrowed in his folded arms. Hearing my footsteps, he lifted his head just enough to snarl, "Go away, Damon. You have your orders."

"It isn't Damon, Mr. Kovacs," I said.

He looked up slowly. "So who is it? Another student wishing to defect? Come to torment me, on the worst day of my life?"

"My name is Nancy Drew," I said firmly. "I'm a friend of George Fayne's."

Kovacs snorted. "So?"

"So—I happen to have done a little detective work. Just a little, here and there. And I couldn't help hearing that you suspect one of your colleagues has been acting unethically. A certain . . . Paul Mourbiers?"

Kovacs froze. "This is possible," he said in a guarded voice.

"I was at the fencing meet yesterday," I told him. "I was watching DeLyn's bout against Una Merrick."

Kovacs stiffened. "And you saw Paul hand her the unstitched gauntlet?" he guessed hopefully.

I shook my head. "No. I wasn't close enough to see the condition of the gauntlet. But I did see how upset DeLyn was when Una got scratched. I can't believe that she would have hurt her opponent on purpose."

Kovacs pursed his lips grimly. "How does this help me, Miss Detective?"

Steeling myself against his rudeness, I said, "We may never know how that gauntlet came open, or when. But maybe we can find out whether Mourbiers set up the interview with the TV reporter. After all, the real problem for you is the publicity. If Mourbiers tricked you into having that fight, knowing it would be covered on TV . . ."

I saw a spark of understanding light up Kovacs's eyes. "You mean he knew they were going to be there?"

"I don't know anything," I said quickly. "But with your permission, I'd like to investigate the possibility."

Kovacs's eyes narrowed. "You want me to pay you to snoop around."

"I never work for money," I hastened to assure him.

Kovacs relaxed. "That's good—because I have no money." Then another thought struck him. "But maybe it is no good to stir up trouble. Our sport is an ancient and·noble one. This is not tacky show biz, like"—here his lip curled in scorn—"*professional wrestling.*"

Seeing me grin, he smiled too. "You may laugh, Miss Detective, but you know what I mean. We fencers have our pride. We have our sense of honor. To make a scandal—it might clear my name, but it would not be good for fencing. And I will do nothing to make fencing look ugly."

"I promise you, I will be discreet," I said. "Whatever information I pick up, I will bring to you, not to the newspapers or to the police. Then you can do with it whatever you feel is right."

Kovacs was actually pleasant looking when he smiled. "I am glad you have come to me, Miss Detective. Miss Nancy Drew. Now I change my mind—perhaps this is not the worst day of my life after all."

"Well, Nancy," said Mr. Nickerson as he climbed into my car later that day, "what sort of trouble are you getting me into now?"

I grinned at Ned's dad. He's a great guy—smart and thoughtful. But he's also the most experienced journalist I know. And for this investigation, he was just the man to help me.

"Who do you know in the news department at the TV station?" I asked.

Mr. Nickerson shrugged. "Lots of people. I know the news director, Dave Markus, pretty well. I don't know too many of the reporters. Some of them think I'm their competition, just because I run the *River Heights Bugle*."

"Aren't you?"

"Not really. Broadcast journalism and print journalism have very different goals. Broadcasters have to entertain their viewers. We newspaper folks are simply committed to informing our readers."

"Even so," I said, "TV reporters ought to be accurate and fair, right?"

"Indeed," Ned's dad agreed.

"In that case," I said, "there's a reporter down there who needs a little talking to." As we drove out to the station, I told him about the unfair coverage of the fencing tournament incident. As I expected, once I appealed to Mr. Nickerson's journalistic ethics, he was eager to help.

The station receptionist recognized Mr. Nickerson and waved us in past the desk. We found the reporter, Kelly Chaffetz, pouring herself a cup of coffee in the newsroom. Standing next to her was a young male reporter wearing a backward baseball cap.

As soon as Mr. Nickerson mentioned the fencing story, Kelly Chaffetz looked guilty. "I know what you're going to say," she said, holding up one hand. "I feel terrible about that story. But we needed something dramatic for that night's newscast, and we had such great footage of that brawl between the two coaches! Time ran out before I could find the second coach, the Hungarian guy, to get his side of the story. My bosses rushed the story onto the air too soon."

The other reporter broke in. "In my opinion, the station should have sent someone from the sports desk. Fencing is a sport, you know."

Kelly Chaffetz flashed him a look of annoyance. "Come on, Derrick. There are fencing tournaments in this area at least once a month, and the sports department was never interested in them before. I figured it was fair territory—a local color feature. All sorts of eccentric people show up for these tournaments. That's what first intrigued me when Mr. Mourbiers called."

Mr. Nickerson and I traded glances. It was just as I had suspected! "Paul Mourbiers called the station and gave you the story idea?" I asked.

Kelly Chaffetz nodded.

Mr. Nickerson gave her his best skeptical editor's frown. "And then you gave him an exclusive on-camera interview afterward to tell his side of the story. Was that ethical?"

She bit her lip. "But I couldn't find the other guy in time!"

Mr. Nickerson put on a look of grave concern. "Is there any chance you'd give Bela Kovacs some airtime another evening, to set the story straight?"

Ms. Chaffetz looked wary. "Possibly. But I'd have to check with my top boss."

"Dave Markus?" Ned's dad said. "Why, he's an old buddy of mine. We used to work in Washington, D.C., together. Could you show me the way to his office? I'd love to stop in and say hi."

Kelly Chaffetz led Mr. Nickerson down a nearby hallway. I was left with the sports reporter. He couldn't wait for his colleague to leave so he could get a word in. "That was so clearly a sports story," he said. "Kelly blew it. Unfortunately, I bet Markus will never agree to put Bela Kovacs on the air. That would make the station look like it's admitting a mistake. He hates to have the station look bad."

I thought fast. "There's another way you could get the truth out," I said. "Do a background story on the history of fencing. That way, you could give Bela Kovacs a chance to appear on camera, looking like an expert instead of a madman. That might help fix his reputation."

The reporter looked interested. "That's a great story idea! I could dig into the archives and see what we've got. We have the best sports videotape archive in the state. We must have some footage of Olympic fencing."

That triggered another idea. "Really? You know, Paul Mourbiers first met Bela Kovacs at the 1976 Olympics—he said so in Kelly's interview. If you could show these two guys back in their Olympic heyday, it would make a perfect local angle." And I'll find out how that feud of theirs got started in the first place, I thought.

The reporter grinned. "You have a real nose for news," he said. "Ever thought about going into journalism? By the way, what's your name?"

An hour later my eyes hurt from staring at grainy videotapes. Derrick and I were sitting in a tiny, windowless room, going through the archives on a small monitor. "It's so much easier with the modern digital tapes." Derrick sighed, hitting the fast-forward button. "You can jump straight to whatever section you need. Rolling through all this is a drag. Why, we must have ninety hours of footage here, just from the '76 Summer Games!"

I sighed too. Ninety hours of tape takes a long time to review, even with a fast-forward button. And we had no guarantee that Bela's bout against Paul Mourbiers had even been included.

"Wait—here's fencing!" Derrick hit the play button.

An announcer's voice came over tiny speakers. "This quarterfinal match should be a crucial one for the Hungarian team. They've been a major fencing power for years, but recently France has been striving to unseat them. Today's match pits Hungary's brightest hope in the épée, Bela Kovacs, against the up-and-coming Frenchman Paul Mourbiers . . ."

"Derrick, this is it!" I said, excited. All our tedious work had paid off!

It was strange to see Kovacs and Mourbiers as skinny young college-age athletes. Bela's curly hair was cut in a short, almost military style, while Paul Mourbiers had a long ponytail. Dressed in white, with their masks down, they were otherwise indistinguishable from each other.

Derrick and I watched the tiny, blurry figures jab and lunge up and down the mat. First Kovacs scored a touch, then Mourbiers. They seemed evenly matched.

The score was tied at fourteen points each. "How many points do you need to win?" Derrick asked.

"Fifteen in a direct elimination bout," I said, pleased that I remembered so much of what Evaline had told me.

And just then I thought I spotted something fishy. "Derrick, stop the tape! Rewind it a few seconds . . . there! Now play." Derrick's finger hovered over the buttons. "Now pause!"

The blurry white figures on the screen froze. "See that?" I said, pointing to the monitor. "When Mourbiers lowers his sword? The tip touched the floor, didn't it?"

Derrick ran the tape back and forth in slow motion, studying it. "It sure looks like it," he agreed. "Is that bad?"

"You can be disqualified," I said, remembering again what Evaline had told me. "But the referee doesn't seem to have seen it."

"Kovacs did," Derrick said. "Look at his reaction. And the way he's staring at the referee, like he expects to hear him call foul on Mourbiers."

"But they're not stopping the bout," I said as the tape rolled on.

"Not only that—they're awarding the point to Mourbiers," Derrick gasped. "That means he wins, right?"

"Just look at that expression on Kovacs's face," I murmured, pausing the tape. "Like his world just fell out from under him."

"Why doesn't he say anything to the referee?" Derrick wondered. "Why doesn't his coach protest? They can't just abide by that bad ruling."

I shook my head. "Different times, maybe. And a different sport. Fencers take pride in being respectful and courteous."

Derrick picked up the printed-out list of Olympic results that had been taped to the videotape case. "It says here that Mourbiers went on to win the semi-final bout, too. He ended up with the silver medal in épée that year."

"That must have made Kovacs furious," I mused.

"But there's an asterisk after his name." Derrick frowned. "That means there was a dispute. Maybe Kovacs did protest after all. Let's fast-forward some more."

Almost at the end of the tape, we found the news report, dated six weeks after the games. "The ruling has come from the Olympic fencing committee: There will be no revision of the medal awards in this summer's Olympic games in Montreal," a news anchor announced. "Hungarian fencer Bela Kovacs lodged a formal protest after his quarterfinal bout against France's Paul Mourbiers, claiming that Mourbiers should have been disqualified for illegally touching his sword tip to the floor. Kovacs backed up his claim with film of the disputed bout. However, the judges said that Kovacs's protest was filed too late."

Next came a head shot of an official from the

international fencing federation, saying in an Italian accent, "By the time we learned of the protest, Monsieur Mourbiers had already won his semifinal bout. At that point, what could we do? We couldn't assume that Kovacs would have won the semifinals if he'd been there instead of Mourbiers. We couldn't replay the semifinals, eh? So we had to let Mourbiers proceed into the finals. It is too bad. The film did show the sword touching the floor. But we cannot reverse the referee's original ruling. Otherwise the Olympic games would be chaos!"

I sat dumbfounded as Derrick stopped the tape. Now everything was painfully clear. "So this is what Bela Kovacs has had to live with," I said. "Just because he didn't protest the referee's judgment soon enough, Mourbiers wasn't disqualified. That's why it riled him up when Mourbiers accused him of rigging the bout. If anyone is a cheater, it's Mourbiers!"

"If I were Kovacs, I'd hate Mourbiers's guts," Derrick added. "Especially when the guy named his studio Salle Olympique! That takes some gall."

I nodded sadly. "Kovacs knows he should have won that bout. He probably could have won the others, too—he could have gone for the gold! And now, for the rest of their lives, Mourbiers can show off his Olympic medal, while Kovacs has nothing."

★ ★ ★ ★

I couldn't wait to tell George what I had learned, so I quickly dropped Mr. Nickerson off and drove straight over to her house. When Mrs. Fayne let me inside, I heard DeLyn's voice upstairs in George's room. Good—I bet she'd be interested in learning how Bela's feud with Paul Mourbiers had started.

"I've heard this story many times from Bela," DeLyn said when I'd finished. She sprang up from George's bed, where the two of them had been relaxing between classes; George was so into fencing, she was up to two a day sometimes. "But you actually saw the videotape? You saw Mourbiers's épée touch the floor?"

"Yup. It was crystal clear," I verified.

"Huh. I always wondered if Bela had just made that up." She scooped up her loafers and slipped them on. "You know, when you tell the same story for years and years, sometimes the facts get a little hazy. Come on, George, we'd better get moving. We don't want to be late for our evening class."

"But how does this change anything?" George asked, fishing around under her bed for her shoes. "If the Olympic committee wouldn't reverse the ruling back then, they're not going to take Paul Mourbiers's medal away now."

"True, we can't fix that for Bela," I admitted. "But if Derrick runs a story explaining the history of their feud, local folks will understand why Bela lost his cool yesterday. Especially when they find out that Paul Mourbiers got Kelly Chaffetz to cover the meet in the first place."

"Anything we can do to ease the tension will help," DeLyn said, striding over to pick up her equipment bag. "We have a college meet coming up this Friday, and nearly half of the fencers train with either Kovacs or Mourbiers. Everybody's taking sides. Things could get nasty."

I hesitated, wondering if DeLyn's brother had told her about Salle Budapest's financial troubles. I bet he hadn't—otherwise she'd have known how badly Bela Kovacs needed to save his reputation, and save it soon.

"Will Damon be fencing in Friday's meet?" George asked, tucking in her T-shirt.

DeLyn frowned, balancing her bag on her shoulder. "Yes. I sure hope he does better this week. He's really been off his form lately. I have no idea why."

I remembered how upset Damon had looked earlier today, when Bela told him about the salle's debts. Could that be affecting his fencing? Damon certainly seemed devoted to his coach.

"Maybe it's just a temporary slump," I suggested.

DeLyn shook her head. "He's been struggling for weeks now. Our coach at school has given him a warning. If Damon can't improve his fencing, he may get cut from the college team."

"But he could still fence for Salle Budapest in noncollege meets," George said, leaning over to pick up her bag.

"If he gets cut from the school team, he'll lose his scholarship," DeLyn explained. "And if he loses his scholarship, he can't afford to stay in college." She paused for a moment. "Hey, I need to do a few things before class. George, I'll come back to pick you up."

After DeLyn left the room, George sighed and said, "She's been so moody lately. I know she's worried about Damon, but she doesn't have to take it out on me!"

I'd been convinced that DeLyn was jealous of Kovacs's praise of George, but maybe I was wrong. Maybe DeLyn was just worried about Damon and his scholarship.

"Ouch!" George exclaimed. She yanked her left hand out of her bag and stuck a finger in her mouth. "Whoo, that hurt!"

"George, are you bleeding?" I said. "What did you touch?"

"Nothing but my foil." George set her bag down and unzipped it all the way. "But the tip of the foil is protected by a guard—it couldn't be sharp. . . ."

Her eyes widened as she extracted the sword from

the bag with her right hand. The long, skinny metal blade quivered as she pulled it free.

"Where did the protective tip go?" George wondered. "I know it was there this afternoon. Those things are soldered on tight—they don't just fall off."

I stepped closer and steadied the flexible blade between my fingers. The pointed end of the blade was etched with tiny scratches, and I could still see a few fragments of solder. The guard was gone and the naked tip shone silver and sharp.

I looked grimly into George's face. "You're right, George—these things don't just fall off. Someone jimmied it off on purpose!"

6

Sabotage!

George lifted her eyes to mine, looking scared. "But who would tamper with my equipment? And why?"

I tested the exposed tip of George's foil with my fingers. "I can't say for sure, George. But I'd say someone could get hurt fencing with a sword in this condition. And if there is a saboteur, I'd bet that would suit him or her just fine."

"George, aren't you ready yet?" said DeLyn, reappearing in the doorway.

"DeLyn, you'd better see this," George said. "Someone removed the tip from my foil."

DeLyn reacted immediately, with a violent start. "*What?* Let me see that!" She dropped her own bag and rushed into George's bedroom.

"It doesn't look accidental," I said as DeLyn inspected George's blade.

"Not a bit," DeLyn agreed, looking worried. "These tips never come off. In all the years I've fenced, I've never seen it happen. Was it loose before, George?"

George shook her head. "I remember touching it this afternoon, and it was on snug. This is a fairly new foil; I just bought it six weeks ago."

Something popped into DeLyn's mind. Dropping George's foil, she dashed to her own bag. Unzipping it, she dug out her foil. Her shoulders sagged with disappointment. She turned and held it up so that George and I could see.

Another naked tip, sharp and shiny.

"So it's not just mine," George said softly.

DeLyn shook her head with a grim expression. "No one's out to hurt *you*, George." She drew a heavy breath. "But it looks like someone *is* out to hurt Salle Budapest."

George looked at me. "Sabotage?"

I nodded. "I'm already on the case. I talked to Bela earlier today. Let me go get my fingerprint kit—I think it's in the trunk of my car."

Usually I try not to let people know when I'm on an investigation. George and Bess and Ned are one thing, but no one else who's involved with a case should know. Not that DeLyn Brittany was a suspect. Of course, I had no reason to clear her name yet, either.

But this was one of those times when I had to show my cards. I needed to take fingerprints off of George's and DeLyn's fencing bags, to see who might have handled them. And I needed to do it right away.

If you've ever watched anybody taking fingerprints, you know you can't do it on the sly. You have to shake this powder all over the area you're checking—in this case, the flat leather areas around the zippers on the fencing bags—and wait a few minutes for print patterns to appear. We ate a quick dinner of warmed-up pizza while we waited. Unfortunately, after the time had passed, I had prints all right—too many prints, from too many different people. And none of them were very clear.

DeLyn scrunched up her nose, looking at the flurry of fingermarks in the powder on her bag. "I guess I never realized how many people touch our bags in the course of an afternoon. We just pile them near the doorway and go fence."

George sighed. "Fencers come, fencers go. You're always moving somebody's bag to get something out of yours. It's chaos."

"Don't worry—it was a long shot," I reassured them. "Even if we did get a clean print, we probably wouldn't have been able to identify our saboteur from it. Most likely whoever did this doesn't have prints on file with the police. Later on, being able to match a fingerprint on the bag might help us prove our case—it would give us concrete evidence to show that person was messing around with the equipment. But it's not likely that a fingerprint would actually lead us to a culprit. Now, let's get the powder cleaned off the bags and go to the salle."

George looked worried. "You want us to go over there and fence? What if other people have had their foils sabotaged like ours? We could get hurt."

"I don't want that to happen," I said. "You'll have to be extremely careful. But we have to find out if other foils were sabotaged. And where else will we learn that?"

George and DeLyn got into George's car and I followed right behind in mine. As I pulled into the Salle Budapest parking lot, I leaned forward to search it. I don't know why, but I suddenly remembered that skinny guy with the ratty jeans who was hanging around the meet yesterday. If anybody fit the image of a deranged saboteur, it was him.

I couldn't see the guy. But a second later, I spotted something equally disturbing—a white van with a small transmitting dish on top, pulling out of the lot and driving away. "Uh-oh," I said to George and

DeLyn after I parked my car and got out. "I'll bet that's the TV station."

"That's good, isn't it?" DeLyn asked. "Wasn't that sports reporter planning to run a follow-up story to repair Bela's image?"

"Yes, but I should have warned Bela someone would be coming."

I looked at George and DeLyn. Their worried expressions confirmed what I had been thinking—that if Bela was caught off guard, he might do something off-the-wall again.

Trying to look as if nothing unusual had happened, DeLyn and George hefted their bags onto their shoulders and marched toward the entrance. I followed close behind. As we went in the front door, I paused to do a quick check of the lock, a simple steel barrel device set into the door frame. "No scratches or dents," I murmured. "No sign that anybody's been trying to break in."

DeLyn tossed a hand dismissively. "That doesn't mean anything. I've never seen that door locked."

"Never?" I was surprised. I mean, I know River Heights isn't what you'd think of as a hotbed of criminal activity, but it gets its share. More than its share, in fact, from what I've seen.

DeLyn nodded. "The salle is almost always open— Bela spends most of his time here. The man has no outside life. He isn't married; he has no family in this country. Technically he lives in a little apartment only a couple of blocks away. But he only goes there to sleep—and some nights, he sleeps here. He keeps a fold-up cot tucked away behind the partition."

George and DeLyn set their bags down carefully, slightly aside from the random heap of gear other fencers had left. I counted only six fencers besides them here tonight—and I could see that DeLyn noticed the number as well. "Generally this clinic has fifteen people enrolled," she murmured. "People are definitely bailing out. Poor Bela!"

I crouched down behind George and DeLyn. "Let me use you guys for cover," I said, reaching surreptitiously for the nearest canvas bag. "People might get mad if they see me rifling through their stuff."

"Sure thing," George said. She and DeLyn spread themselves out as much as possible, which wasn't hard, considering all the fencing gear they had to put on—plastic chest guards, padded tunics, gloves, and steel-mesh masks.

Damon Brittany strolled over from the fencing floor, his mask under his arm. "Where were you guys?" he asked, sounding annoyed. "Did you go somewhere for dinner? I was afraid you were going to miss the clinic."

DeLyn threw him a get-out-of-my-face type of

look. "We just went to George's house for a break. I can't spend every minute of my life at the salle, Damon—not like some folks I know." She turned her back on him while she strapped on her chest protector.

Damon crouched down on the floor next to her bag. "You don't have to get so touchy," he complained. "I just wondered what you did for dinner."

"Leftover pizza at my place—you didn't miss anything," George told him.

I shifted quietly away from them. No point in letting Damon notice I was going through other fencers' bags. It was bad enough that DeLyn knew I was working on the case. I just hoped she had enough sense not to tell her brother.

As soon as Damon went back to fencing, I unzipped the first bag. My heart sank as I pulled out a foil. The protective tip on this one was gone, just like George's and DeLyn's. The same evidence of fresh tampering was all over the blade. I silently set the foil aside, making sure it was properly labeled with its owner's name before I separated it from its bag.

The next two bags I checked, however, had no foils in them. I sat on my heels, puzzled.

Then, looking toward the studio floor, I realized why there were no foils in the bags. The fencers had their foils in hand—and they were dueling with them already! "Doesn't anybody check their equipment before fencing?" I groaned. "We've got to stop them before someone's hurt." I stood up and headed toward the fencing area.

"Hold it, Nancy. Go tell Bela," George said, lifting her mask to look at me. "Let him be the one to stop the class. If you do it, everyone will know you're a detective."

George was right. If I blew my cover, I wouldn't be able to investigate quietly anymore. I collected the three foils—George's, DeLyn's, and the third one I'd just found—and walked the length of the studio, heading for the office cubicles at the far end. Since Bela wasn't in sight, I figured he was back behind the partition. Like DeLyn had said, he was always somewhere at the salle.

As I got closer to the partition, I heard a low voice that I recognized as belonging to one of the assistant teachers. Bela's voice, edged with harshness, replied sharply, "Tear up that message slip. Tear it up! If anybody from the bank calls again, say I'm not in. Understand? I don't want to talk to any of those so-called loan officers. Hah! Sharks is what they are. Sharks with many rows of sharp teeth! What else do you need to bother me about?"

The assistant murmured something I couldn't

make out. I stole closer, ducking down behind the nearest partition.

Bela snapped back, "George Fayne? Oh, pair her up with one of the other beginners. She's hardly worth our time. We'll never make a fencer out of her—not like DeLyn."

"But Bela," the assistant protested, "just the other day I heard you call George your star of the future."

"And when I said that, wasn't DeLyn standing there too?" Bela replied.

"Why . . . yes, come to think of it. . . ."

"So?" Kovacs said brusquely. "I had to do something to wake up DeLyn. I need to help her get her competitive juices flowing again. I thought a little jealousy might do the trick."

I felt my stomach flip. So that's what the crafty old fencing master had been up to! He was playing George and DeLyn—two friends!—off each other.

I began to back away from the cubicle. At that moment, I was so steamed up, I didn't want to talk to Bela Kovacs. So what if a saboteur was putting all his students in danger? He deserved it, the rotten old guy!

But at that very moment Bela came charging around the partition, pulling up the suspenders of his fencing breeches. He saw me standing there with the three foils in my hand, their naked tips held out in front. As he stared at them his face turned pale.

"Miss Drew!" he said nervously. "Where did you get those?"

"From the bags of three different fencers," I said quietly. "Bags that were lying around in the salle this afternoon."

"Shhh!" He grabbed me by the arm and pulled me back into his private cubicle. "No one must know!"

I frowned. "You knew this already and you didn't tell anyone?"

Bela's shoulders sagged. "During the dinner break, I noticed the same thing was done to several of the salle's house weapons—the ones we lend out when fencers forget theirs. I put them away at once, so no one would use them. I hoped I had already found all the problem foils." He ran a hand over his face. "I planned to stay up all night, soldering new tips on so they'd be back in shape by tomorrow. Give me those three foils and I'll fix them, too."

"I'm not worried about getting them fixed," I said. "What worries me is that some of those fencers may be fighting with unprotected foils right now!"

Bela's eyes flicked nervously in the direction of the fencing area. "Yes, yes, yes . . . I'd better stop them. I'll tell Ted—we'll get out plastic swords instead. There's an exercise we do sometimes with the plastic swords. . . ."

He headed out of the cubicle but turned back for a moment. "Please, Miss Drew, I beg of you: *Do not let anyone know this has happened*. We had two new students here this afternoon, and I cannot afford for them to be scared away!"

I couldn't help but nod in agreement. I'd been so mad just a minute ago, but I could tell how much the idea of sabotage upset Bela.

Bela was gone for only a minute. When he came back into the cubicle, he looked shaken. He had five foils, which he'd retrieved from the other students. Without a word, he held them up for me to look at. All of them had bare tips.

Bela sank wearily into his desk chair. "Thank goodness I sent those people from the television away," he moaned. "They showed up tonight with no warning! The man said he was going to film a follow-up to yesterday's story—tell my side of the story. Hah!" He threw up his hands.

Then Bela's eyes widened. He grabbed the hair on either side of his head and pulled it furiously. "Paul Mourbiers must be behind this! I am certain of it. He sent a spy here to plant evidence—to make me look bad again. Then he got the news reporters to come so they would find out about it. Such evil!"

"Now, wait, Mr. Kovacs," I said. "I was the one who convinced that reporter to do a follow-up story.

I thought it would help you to tell your side of the story. Paul Mourbiers had nothing to do with it—at least not this time."

Bela didn't look convinced. "But he must have tampered with our swords. Who else could have done it?"

My stomach stirred uneasily. "You said you had two new students today?"

Bela's eyes met mine, guessing at once what I suspected. "Mourbiers's spies!"

Even though I'd had the same idea, Bela Kovacs seemed way too quick to blame his rival.

"Let me go get their names from the sign-in sheet," he said, jumping up from his desk. "I think I can give you a description of them too. Unfortunately, we don't ask for addresses or phone numbers. But I bet if you go to Salle Olympique tomorrow, you'll find the same two traitors fencing there."

Just as he turned to leave the cubicle, an anguished cry broke out on the salle floor. I couldn't be sure, but it sounded like DeLyn.

Bela Kovacs raced to the open fencing area. I was right behind him. As we came out from behind the partition, I could see a fencer in white, writhing on the floor.

It wasn't DeLyn—although she was kneeling right next to the body, mouth still open from her scream. I was relieved to see George standing beside her, unscathed. But who could the hurt fencer be? I couldn't see the face behind the wire-mesh mask.

The figure on the floor flailed about frantically, moaning and whimpering in pain. DeLyn leaned forward, tugging at the person's mask. "Are you okay?" she asked. "Speak to me, Damon!"

7

A Whiff of Danger

DeLyn fumbled frantically with the Velcro straps securing her twin brother's fencing mask. Bela Kovacs gently pushed her aside, undid Damon's mask in one swift motion, and lifted it free. Damon's eyes were screwed shut and his face was contorted with pain.

Bela handed me the mask. An overpowering smell hit me. A sweet perfumy odor—but underneath, the piercing chemical scent of ammonia. I recognized it from the strong cleaners Hannah sometimes used. But what was ammonia doing on Damon's fencing mask?

"Quick, get him to a sink so he can run water over his face!" I said. I knew that if the ammonia came into contact with his skin, it could irritate or even burn him. Flushing it immediately with cold water was the only solution.

Bela already had a firm grip on Damon's elbow and was pulling him to his feet. Hunched over and stumbling, Damon let himself be guided to the restroom. George had already run back there to start filling the sink, so by the time Damon got there, the basin was full of fresh, cold water. He bent over and plunged his face in.

"Aarghh!" Damon raised his head and cried out, as if the cold water hurt his skin. But he plunged it in again.

A circle of anxious fencers had gathered, crowding around the bathroom door. "Show's over, folks," Bela called out, clapping his hands. "Get back to your drills!" But he kept a hand on Damon's back, patting him and reassuring him.

"It's nothing, really, Bela," Damon said, lifting his dripping face from the sink. "I guess I just got a little too much cleaning fluid on my mask. Could you give it here?"

I looked down and realized I was still holding Damon's mask. He snatched it away from me.

DeLyn frowned. "Cleaning fluid?"

Damon hiked up one shoulder defensively. "The wire mesh was getting crudded up. I needed to scour it clean. By accident, I must have used too much. No big deal!" He tucked the mask behind his back.

I'd had a split second to look at the mask, and in that moment I'd seen that the name, written in black marker on the mask's white canvas straps, was DeLyn's, not Damon's. Odd.

If Damon claimed he had put cleaning fluid on his own mask, how come DeLyn's mask was the one that smelled like ammonia?

Somebody wasn't telling the straight story. And I had to find out who.

I walked back to the front of the studio, to where the fencers piled their belongings during class. My eyes swept the pale, polished wood floor in search of clues.

"Can I borrow a mask from the cupboard, Bela?" I heard Damon ask behind me. "Until this one airs out?"

"You're not going back on the floor, Damon," Bela replied gruffly. "You take the rest of the evening off."

"But Bela—," Damon began to protest.

"No argument," Bela said curtly. "You're finished with class for tonight. DeLyn, you go too. Take your brother home."

That's when I spied a tiny scrap of something shiny and wet-looking on the floor. I knelt down to swipe at it with my finger. It was a soft, transparent scrap of plastic gel, called an ampoule. It's a casing for medicine, like the outside of a capsule. Where had I seen one before?

Then I remembered—in a first-aid kit. Every coach has on hand a few ampoules of ammonium carbonate, commonly called smelling salts. If someone is knocked unconscious, you break open the ampoule under the person's nose to release the stimulant scent. It brings them back to consciousness in a hurry. Getting hold of an ammonium carbonate ampoule would be easy. I could see at once how it had been done—the ampoule fastened loosely inside the mask, so that it would break open the minute the fencer pulled his mask into place. And once that smell was released . . .

"Come on, Damon," I heard DeLyn say as she unzipped her tunic. "Let's call it a day. You know how slow the buses run on Wednesday nights, anyway."

"No bus," Bela commanded. "Miss Drew, you drive them home."

I flashed Bela Kovacs a puzzled look, but I didn't argue. Whether or not he intended to, Bela was giving me the perfect opportunity to interrogate the Brittany twins and to sneak a closer look at that mask.

I tried to make my voice sound as casual as possible. "No problem. I've got my car outside. And you're on my way."

Damon frowned as he started to strip off his gear. "How do you know we're on your way? You don't even know where we live."

I had to backpedal, fast. Sure, I didn't know where they lived. But they didn't know where I lived either. Theoretically, anywhere could be on my way. "Don't you live on campus?" I asked, for starters.

Damon shook his head. "Too expensive. We still live at home with our mom. We're way over on the west side."

"That's fine," I said. It really was the opposite direction from my house. But the Brittany twins didn't need to know that.

"Oh, and Damon?" Bela called out from the fencing floor. "I won't charge you for tonight's class. Consider it a freebie."

Damon looked relieved. "Thanks, Bela."

I was surprised by that bit of conversation. From what I had gathered, money was fairly tight for the twins. And at their level, they must be taking several classes a week. It hadn't occurred to me that Bela charged them for every lesson they took. Once we were driving away from the salle, I asked, as casually as possible, "I thought you guys were the stars of Salle Budapest. Does Bela still charge you for lessons?"

DeLyn jumped in quickly. "Oh, no, not full price. We get a discount for taking so many lessons a week.

And then he gives us part-time jobs—answering phones while we're at the salle, that sort of thing, and it helps us pay our lesson bill."

"Bela's been great, just great," Damon echoed his sister. "He does everything he can to make it affordable for us. Of course, we still have to buy all our equipment."

"And we have to go to a lot of tournaments, some of them pretty far away," DeLyn explained. "But if we don't compete, we can't keep up our national rankings. And those rankings helped us get our college scholarships. Right, Damon?"

Damon grunted a brief reply. It seemed to be a touchy subject with him right now.

"Mom's had to work a lot of extra nursing shifts at the hospital to keep up with all the costs," DeLyn admitted. "But she always says it's worth it. And she never complains about paying Bela. After all, he needs to make a living too. Bela's lessons are worth every penny we pay."

"He's been like a second father to us," Damon said earnestly. "Our father died when we were seven years old. It's been up to Mom to support us ever since."

"My mom died when I was three," I told them. I felt a tug of sympathy, knowing that Damon and DeLyn were half orphans like me. But even so, I knew that my situation was different. I had had the warmhearted Hannah Gruen to fill in for my mother. All the twins had was gruff, demanding Bela Kovacs.

The Brittany home was a small, neat, white frame bungalow on a crowded block of small bungalows, some of them more run-down than others. "Was Mom working late tonight, Damon?" DeLyn asked as we pulled up to the curb.

"I forget. I can't keep track of her crazy work schedule," her brother replied.

The twins didn't invite me to come in, but I switched off the engine and went up the walk with them anyway. I figured they'd have to let me inside once we got to the door. "Mom, we're home!" DeLyn called out as she unlocked the door.

"My, my, aren't you home early?" a voice called out from a back room.

Damon flashed DeLyn a fierce warning glare. I guessed he didn't want her to tell his mother about the incident at the salle. "A friend gave us a ride," DeLyn called back. "We didn't have to wait for the bus, that's all."

Once inside, I felt like I was in a museum, not a home. Every square inch of wall was occupied with framed award certificates and photos of the twins in fencing costume. Every spare shelf and tabletop was loaded with trophies. "Wow!" I exclaimed. "Between the two of you, you must have won every prize at every tournament you ever attended."

Damon winced and turned aside. "I'm gonna take a shower," he said abruptly. "My skin is still stinging." He crossed the living room in two strides and disappeared.

"I'll be right back," DeLyn murmured, looking anxious. She hurried after her brother, leaving me in the living room alone. Unfortunately, she carried her equipment bag with her. How was I going to get a look at that ammonia-tainted mask?

At least there was plenty to look at while I waited. Some of the photographs showed DeLyn and Damon as kids, clutching trophies and grinning. Bela Kovacs appeared in a lot of those early pictures, beaming as he posed with his prize students. The older they got, the less often Bela was in the photos. And, I began to realize, as they got older more pictures featured DeLyn, not Damon. I began to read the brass plaques on the trophies and medals. In recent years DeLyn's trophies outnumbered her brother's.

"We sure have a lot of hardware here to look at," I heard Mrs. Brittany's voice behind me. I turned around and smiled. A short, plump woman, Mrs. Brittany was still dressed in her nurse's uniform—not the crisp starched white of a registered nurse, but the blue and white stripes of a less trained (and not as well paid) practical nurse. She came shuffling into the living room, walking as though her feet hurt. I know how much time nurses spend on their feet; I felt bad for her, watching her slowly make her way over to an armchair.

"The twins are really champions, aren't they?" I replied.

"Oh, yes, I'm mighty proud of them," Mrs. Brittany said with a huge grin. "Are you one of their fencing friends?"

"Sort of," I said. "I met them at Salle Budapest. But I'm not a fencer myself; I was just there with one of my friends. My name is Nancy Drew."

"Pleased to meet you, Miss Drew." Mrs. Brittany waved, but she didn't get up from her chair to shake hands. Sitting down was too much of a relief, I guessed.

DeLyn popped back into the room, giving me frantic looks and holding a finger to her lips. Obviously she didn't want me to tell her mother about Damon's accident. Glancing over at Mrs. Brittany, weary from her extra shifts, I decided to follow DeLyn's advice, at least for the moment. "I was just admiring your trophies, DeLyn," I said. "Do you and Damon keep a running score of who has the most?"

DeLyn flinched. Clearly I had hit a sore spot. Well,

good—sometimes hitting a sore spot can make people tell you things you need to know. "I think Damon faces tougher competition than I do," DeLyn said loyally.

"No, don't you be modest, Lyn," Mrs. Brittany chided her. "You've worked so hard to get that high ranking of yours. Damon's got to hustle to keep up. Would you believe, Miss Drew, that Damon was the one who started fencing first? I don't know how he got the notion to take up fencing—he was just a little boy, nine or so. DeLyn was still taking ballet classes, weren't you, honey? The community center offered lots of free classes for little kids back then. Two years later, Bela saw Damon at a junior meet and asked him to study at the salle. Being a single mom, I thought it would be easier if I could send both children to the same activity, so we persuaded DeLyn to go to fencing class too. And oh, my, how fast she took off! Bela says she has a natural gift."

DeLyn frowned. "But Damon's still an excellent fencer."

"Of course, honey. I was so thrilled when you both got those scholarships. I don't know how we would have scraped together the money for college without that. But you're Bela's star. You're the one he's always asking to do public fencing demonstrations, like at the mall two weeks ago."

"Just because he needs to attract more girls to the salle," DeLyn said. "If they see a girl fencing, they can imagine themselves doing it. Nancy, can I get you a cold drink? Come into the kitchen." Clearly, this line of discussion made her uncomfortable.

In the small, bright kitchen, I asked, "How's Damon feeling?"

DeLyn sighed. "Physically, just fine. But he's in a rotten mood. Lately it seems he's always in a rotten mood. Especially at the salle—Bela is constantly on his case."

"Bela can be a difficult guy," I said, hoping to get DeLyn to open up.

DeLyn opened the refrigerator door, but she just stood there for a minute, as if she had forgotten what she was looking for. "He's been on my case too. He's so demanding—he expects me to win every bout I fence! And there's Damon, sitting on the sidelines, watching me win and feeling jealous." She leaned against the refrigerator door, lost in thought. "And that makes Damon feel even worse—he feels guilty about being jealous of me. You don't understand what it's like to be a twin, Nancy—we're closer than most brothers and sisters. He's not just my brother, he's my best friend. Can you blame me if sometimes I lose, just to make him feel better?"

So that was it! "Have you told Bela that you're throwing some bouts on purpose?" I asked.

She shook her head as she took out a pitcher of lemonade. "Bela wouldn't understand. He lives and dies to compete, that old fox. You've seen the way he is with Paul Mourbiers—and how many years has it been since they fenced against each other? No, he'd have no sympathy for me losing on Damon's account." She poured two glasses of lemonade.

"But don't those losses affect your ranking?" I asked.

She wrinkled her nose. "Yes. I try to lose only in events that aren't sanctioned by the national organization, so it won't be factored in. But the coach of the university team keeps track all the same. I have to play it carefully—I can't afford to lose that scholarship." Her eyes welled up with tears.

"I know you're worried about Damon losing his scholarship," I said sympathetically. "But yours, too?"

DeLyn set down the pitcher and lowered her voice. "My scholarship isn't in the same danger To tell you the truth, Nancy . . . Damon's always been a borderline case with the school team. They didn't offer him the scholarship right away—not until I was in the final stages of accepting mine. You know, I almost went to another school, where the scholarship paid even more. Then the university offered Damon a scholarship too. That sealed my decision to go there."

"Do you think they only gave one to Damon to attract you?" I asked.

DeLyn hesitated, then nodded again. "Most days, I don't know who I'm fencing for," she said. "For Bela, so he can show me off as his prize pupil? For my mom, so she can believe all the sacrifices were worth it? Or for Damon, so he doesn't feel inferior?"

She lowered her head, wiping her eyes. "I'm sure not doing it for the love of fencing anymore. It seems like my whole life has been devoted to this sport—and now it's killing me!"

8

The Other Side

I **was still brooding** about DeLyn the next morning, as George and I got into my car and drove the twenty miles to Cutler Falls. "It would be a pain to drive this far every time you wanted to take a fencing lesson," George remarked. "In the end, I don't think students will defect from Salle Budapest if they have to go all the way to Salle Olympique."

"I don't know," I said, thinking of how unhappy some folks at Salle Budpest were—including its brightest star. "Some people might think it was worth the drive. Especially fencers who got the impression that Bela Kovacs is a lunatic."

"It's too bad he didn't let Derrick inside to do that follow-up story yesterday," George said. "The sooner his public image is corrected, the better. Any student who's worked with him knows the real Bela."

I stole a sideways glance at her. She really seemed convinced. But the Bela Kovacs she thought she knew was very different from the Bela Kovacs that Ned Nickerson knew. Different also from the Bela who was making Damon and DeLyn so miserable. So which one was the real Bela Kovacs?

I looked away, feeling a little guilty. I hadn't told George about the conversation I had heard yesterday—about how Bela had only been puffing up her ego in order to goad DeLyn. I didn't have the heart to tell George what he really thought of her.

"What do you think was the deal with Damon's mask yesterday?" George asked, changing the subject.

"I don't know," I said. "We've got to figure Damon lied, though. He said he used cleaning fluid on his mask, right? But I was holding that mask he wore— it was DeLyn's mask, George. It had her name all over it."

George's eyes grew round. "Wow. So does that mean somebody was trying to hurt DeLyn?"

"It looks like it to me," I said. "After all, she is the salle's most prominent fencer, isn't she? If someone wanted to make the salle look bad, it would be logical to go after DeLyn. She had one of the tampered foils in her bag. The incident at the tournament the other day occurred in DeLyn's bout too."

"It's got to be Paul Mourbiers," George said. "He's the one who hates Bela. He's the one who has most to gain if Salle Budapest goes under."

I shook my head. "I wish it were that simple. Paul Mourbiers might have had access to Una's gauntlet at the meet the other day, but how would he have gotten into Salle Budapest to damage so many foils? And DeLyn's mask? It was in her bag when she was at your house yesterday. You had more opportunity to tamper with it than Mourbiers did."

George frowned. "What are you saying, Nancy?"

"Don't worry, George," I said, smiling. "You're not on my suspect list. I'm just saying that I don't see Salle Olympique as our chief suspect anymore."

George looked out the window. "So Mourbiers must have sent spies. That's why we're going to Cutler Falls now—to find them, right?"

"Perhaps," I said. "We have to check out that possibility, but there's no guarantee that yesterday's students have anything to do with Salle Olympique."

"What about that scruffy-looking guy you were telling me about?" George asked. "You know for sure he was at Salle Budapest a couple of times, plus he was at the meet. Maybe *he's* working for Mourbiers."

"Maybe," I agreed. "But it's hard to believe that Mourbiers would hire somebody who so obviously stands out to do his undercover dirty work. If that guy went inside Salle Budapest, they'd throw him out before he had a chance to tamper with any equipment."

"You have a point," George admitted.

I paused, reluctant to bring up my next line of reasoning. "George . . . do you think Bela Kovacs himself could be responsible?"

"No way!" George replied hotly. "He wouldn't sabotage his own salle! It's not just his business—it's his life."

I hesitated. I knew George wasn't exactly impartial. And I needed an impartial ear right now. But I also knew that George was just as determined to get to the bottom of this case as I was. She wouldn't be able to ignore the facts of the case, no matter how closely she was involved with the suspects. "Maybe it isn't the salle he's trying to sabotage," I suggested gently. "Maybe it's just one person at the salle."

George sat up straight. "You mean DeLyn? Oh, no, Nancy, you're way off base. DeLyn is his star student, everybody knows that. Bela made her the champion fencer she is today. If she looks bad, he looks bad. He can't afford that."

"But DeLyn says he's been so critical of her lately," I pointed out. "He says rude things to her all the time, and she hasn't been winning the way he expects her to. Look, George, all I know is that Damon was lying about his mask yesterday. Clearly he's covering up for someone. And he's very loyal to Bela Kovacs—more loyal than DeLyn is. If Damon suspected Bela was after his sister . . ."

"I don't buy it, Nancy," George replied with a stubborn look. "Damon is devoted to Bela, but he's even more devoted to DeLyn. If Damon knew someone was out to hurt his twin, he certainly wouldn't sit back and let it happen."

I sighed. "Too true. That's why this case is so mind-boggling."

Salle Olympique looked amazingly like Salle Budapest. It was located in the same kind of commercial lot, with a similar blacktop parking lot and nondescript weedy borders. It was the same type of one-story cinder-block building, with a tan brick front wall and a large front window. Paul Mourbiers had even painted the name of his salle in the same curlicue red and black letters. "It looks like an exact clone of Salle Budapest," I said, astonished.

George grinned wryly. "Well, to tell you the truth, it's the other way around—Salle Budapest is an exact clone of Salle Olympique. Remember, Mourbiers opened his studio six years ago. Back then, Bela Kovacs was in a run-down space downtown. He borrowed tons of money to build a new facility to compete with Mourbiers, and he made it look exactly like the rival salle. Sort of a dig at Mourbiers, I guess."

I shook my head as I parked the car. "I swear, from everything I hear about their rivalry, I don't know which of them acts worse."

"Let's hope no one recognizes us from before," George said, climbing out of the car.

"I'd thought of that, too—but we've got to take the chance. We'll just lay low."

Paul Mourbiers himself was sitting at the front desk when we walked into the all-too-familiar-looking studio. "Do you have to be registered ahead if you want to take a class?" George asked. "We've never fenced before, but we'd like to try it out."

"We saw something on the TV news a couple of nights ago that made us curious," I added.

Mourbiers's face lit up at the mention of the TV news report. "Yes, yes, walk-ins are always welcome," he declared. "Just sign in here." He pushed a clipboard toward us. "We are always happy to introduce new students to the honorable and ancient art of fencing."

"Yeah—honorable," George said, barely hiding her sarcastic tone. The way she was studying Paul Mourbiers, I felt sure he'd guess we weren't just innocent beginners. But Mourbiers seemed oblivious to her hostility—he was just glad to have some new students. And when I wrote down my address on his sign-in sheet, he beamed even more.

"You are from River Heights!" he exclaimed.

"Yes," I said, busily scanning the rest of the sign-in sheet for the names Bela had given me. "I know there's a fencing school in our town, but we heard better things about yours. That's why we drove over to try you out."

Mourbiers rubbed his hands together. "Excellent," he crooned. "We can lend you the necessary equipment for today, of course. Why don't you step over this way?" He gestured toward the equipment closet, which lined the side wall, just like at Salle Budapest. "Anton, get these new students suited up. I personally will handle their instruction—just to make sure they begin on the best possible foot."

"Were those names there?" George muttered in my ear as we followed Mourbiers's assistant instructor, Anton.

"Nope," I said. "But they may have written down false names on the sheet at Salle Budapest, like we just did. As far as Salle Olympique knows, my name is Daphne Gherkin."

George grinned. "I saw. And I'm Phoebe Karabell."

"Nice to meet you, Phoebe."

"Nice to meet you, Daph."

On the fencing floor, I quickly realized that it was going to be hard to tell if the "spies" were here. Most fencers had their masks on, covering their faces. Bela had told me that one of the suspicious new students was a sixteen-year-old guy with bright red hair, and I couldn't see any redheads among Mourbiers's students this morning. The other fencer Bela suspected was a tall, broad-shouldered girl of about fourteen, with a brown ponytail. I tried to maneuver around the studio to check out the other fencers' hair, while George kept Mourbiers distracted by asking lots of questions. "Why do fencers say 'On guard'?" she asked.

"It's a French phrase—*en garde*," he said, dramatically rolling the *r*. "France, you know, is the country where fencing reached its highest flower. When a fencer says, *En garde*, it is to warn his or her opponent to prepare to fight. You hold your sword straight up like this and crouch down in a fighting posture. No, no, bend your knees more, and angle your body like so. You are exposing too much of your front toward me. Come at me with your shoulder only."

"But if you're trying to win, why give them a warning?" George asked.

"Because fencing is a sport of chivalry," Mourbiers replied, sounding offended. "It would not be proper to fight someone who was not ready to parry your blade."

"Parry?"

"Yes, a parry is a move to knock your opponent's blade aside. Like so." He swiftly flicked up the foil he was holding and fended off George's loosely dangling foil.

I sidled down the studio, noticing a bulletin board at the far end. I figured there was a good chance that Mourbiers's "spies" weren't here this morning—but they might be enrolled in other classes at other times. Now, if George could only keep Mourbiers busy, I'd have a chance to examine the lists. Behind me I could hear George clanging her borrowed sword against the master's. *"Touché!"* Mourbiers called out.

"I've heard that in cartoons and stuff," said George. "What does that mean?"

"It simply means that you have been touched by your opponent's sword. That is a point for me. If we were scoring, I would be ahead."

"Well, *touché* yourself!" I heard George's foot stomp as she lunged toward Mourbiers. But there was an answering ring of metal on metal. "That move is called a feint," Mourbiers explained. "I look like I'm going to move one way, but instead I move another—"

Just then, across the studio, a heavy saber clattered to the floor.

And I whipped around to see a young woman fencer writhing and clutching at her white doublet, crying out in pain.

9

Suspected

As I raced toward her, I saw that the fencer was yanking hard at the electrical cord plugged into the lower hem of her silvery lamé. It took two hands for her to disconnect the plug. The minute it was detached, she groaned and slumped in relief.

"Are you all right?" Paul Mourbiers asked her, frowning with concern.

She reached up and pulled off her mask. Even in her distress, she was careful to fluff her short strawberry blond hair back into place. I stifled a gasp. I recognized her, all right—it was Una, the fencer DeLyn had faced in Tuesday's disastrous bout. Even now, as she stripped off her doublet, I could see the gauze taped to her forearm where DeLyn's foil had jabbed her.

Mourbiers had the electronic scoring leash in his hand. He touched the metal prongs at the end. I was close enough to see that the copper wires were shining, exposed, below the plug. It looked as if someone had cut away the black rubber coating that insulated the wires leading to the plug!

I had seen enough of the equipment at Salle Budapest to know how it worked. The electrical impulse distributed a mild current to the metallic threads in the lamé—enough to register a touch from a metal sword and send a signal to the scoring device. The underside of the lamé, however, had a layer of insulation so the fencer would not feel any electric shock.

But with the wires exposed, Una had accidentally touched a live electrical current with her bare hands. I remembered once touching a frayed lamp cord and feeling a current buzz through my body. I'd felt like my whole body was lighting up. I wasn't badly hurt, but my heart had thumped hard and my body had tingled for several minutes. Looking at Una, her eyes wide and her breathing rapid, I could imagine she was feeling the same unpleasant effect—maybe even worse, having held the live wires longer.

Now that Mourbiers noticed the exposed wires, his dark eyes narrowed with anger. "Sabotage!" he hissed, pronouncing the word with a nasty flourish.

I exchanged a worried look with George. Surely an electrical cord could be worn to pieces on its own. So why did Mourbiers jump to the conclusion that there was foul play involved?

"And I know who is behind it," the French fencing master went on ominously. "Bela Kovacs."

Una looked at him fearfully. "Paul, do you really think . . . ?"

Mourbiers pounded a fist into his other palm. "The mad Hungarian. Of course! How could I not see it coming? First he damages your gauntlet at the meet. Now this. Una, you are a threat to his precious DeLyn Brittany. She will not be on top forever; you are challenging her now, and Kovacs doesn't like it. He *does not like it one bit.*"

I looked over at George, who was quivering with the effort it took not to speak out in defense of Bela Kovacs. I steadied her with a glance. Then I reached over and grabbed the cord out of Mourbiers's hand. I deliberately pressed my fingers against the live wires, drawing the shock into myself. "That little zap?" I said. "That's hardly worth worrying about. Sure, it took you by surprise. But it's not going to do any real damage."

George, taking her cue from me, chimed in. "You're right, Daphne," she said. "Why, if I were going to sabotage somebody, I'd do something really

mean—like taking the safety tips off their swords."
She darted a rude glance at Mourbiers.

Mourbiers drew himself up to his full height and
looked down his elegant hawklike nose at us.
"Clearly you do not comprehend. It is not physical
damage I complain of. It is psychological damage. A
fencer of Una's quality is like a thoroughbred race-
horse—she must not be discomposed. Her courage
must not be tampered with—especially not the day
before a big meet." He stabbed the air with his forefinger. "I cannot have my top woman fencer nervous
and jumpy every time she puts on a lamé! Only an
experienced fencer would understand this effect.
Only a fencing master would know how effective
this sort of sabotage could be. Only Bela Kovacs
would be capable of such a low deed!"

"Who's this Bela Kovacs?" I asked, playing dumb.

But Paul Mourbiers was just as paranoid as Bela
Kovacs. Once the idea of sabotage was in his head,
there was no shaking it. "You two know perfectly
well who Bela Kovacs is!" he thundered. "I know
every other fencer in this room—but not you two.
You show up out of the blue, and suddenly a thing
like this happens. It is no coincidence, I can assure
you! Kovacs has sent you—to bring about my ruin!"

If we hadn't been personally under attack, I guess I
would have seen Mourbiers's hysterical reaction as

pretty ridiculous. But you tend not to laugh in the face of someone who's furiously brandishing a sword at you. "Come on, Phoebe," I muttered to George.

"Now I recognize you!" Mourbiers went on, pointing that accusing forefinger straight at George. "You were fencing for Salle Budapest on Tuesday! I remember watching you lose your bout—spectacularly, I might add. You had terrible footwork, rotten timing, a weak attack. And of course, being badly coached by Bela Kovacs, you will never improve. You are a clumsy amateur—and you are a saboteur! Get out of my salle, and get out now!"

George and I had already dropped our foils and were heading for the door.

"And if you ever dare to darken my doors again, I will call the police on you!" Mourbiers called after us.

George and I were both pretty eager to put Cutler Falls and Salle Olympique behind us, and fast. We scuttled out the door and got into my car. But things always go wrong at the worst times. When I tried to start my car . . .

"Oh, no, Nancy," George groaned. "Don't tell me. You forgot to charge up your car again!"

Now, I love my hybrid car. It makes me very happy to know that I am not wasting scarce petroleum resources or polluting the environment with car emissions (plus I save plenty of money on gas). But there is one disadvantage of driving a hybrid: If you don't plug the battery in every once in a while, it runs down. And—well, sometimes when I'm absorbed with a case, I just forget to hook it up at night. Usually the car charges up when you drive it on the highway and it switches over to the gasoline-powered mode. But driving to Cutler Falls, we hadn't been on any highway. Apparently we hadn't been going fast enough to kick into the gasoline power. And now my battery was flat as a pancake.

"I'd better phone Charlie to give me a boost." I pulled out my cell phone.

"Couldn't you call a local garage?" George asked. "I mean, it'll take Charlie twenty minutes to get over here from River Heights. And, uh, it would be nice to get out of here sooner than that." She cast an uneasy look back at the Salle Olympique building.

But I had already dialed Charles Adams's number. And I have to admit, I was too embarrassed to call anybody else. Charlie wouldn't tease me. Charlie never teases me, and he always comes as soon as I call.

George rolled her eyes. "Must be nice to have the best mechanic in River Heights have such a crush on you."

Charlie said he would come right away, of course. In fact, he'd been out somewhere in his truck and was already halfway to Cutler Falls. George and I leaned against my car, waiting, trying not to notice that Paul Mourbiers kept coming to the window of the salle to glare at us.

"I can't believe Mourbiers went crazy on us like that," George said. "There's no proof that that damaged electrical lead was intentionally sabotaged. Who would want to hurt Una? She's really not much of a threat to DeLyn; DeLyn has beaten her many times in competition."

I shrugged. "Paul Mourbiers is just as crazy as Bela when it comes to their rivalry," I said. "I don't trust a word either one of them says anymore. They're too paranoid. At this point, I'm beginning to doubt that either salle is sabotaging the other one."

"Then how do you explain everything?" George asked. "There have been too many 'accidents' lately. I have to believe one person is behind them all. And who else but Paul Mourbiers would have a motive?"

But by then, I wasn't really listening to George. I was peering intently at the scrubby trees and tall weeds at the edge of the parking lot.

There he was—the scuzzy guy in the old overcoat. Raggedy Man, I called him in my mind. It couldn't be just a coincidence that he was here today, loitering at the edge of the parking lot. First the tournament on Tuesday, now here today—following a trail of damaged equipment and injured fencers . . .

Now George saw Raggedy Man too. "Should we grill him?" she asked.

"I don't know," I admitted, shifting my weight from foot to foot. "I'd hate to scare him off before we see what he's doing. So long as he doesn't know we're watching, he may do something—something definite, to give us solid proof that he's up to no good."

I cast another nervous look toward Salle Olympique to see if Mourbiers was still staring out at us. The person I saw instead was Una, walking out the front door of the building. She had changed into her street clothes, stylish tailored trousers and a matching sweater set. She carried her fencing bag tightly by the short handles, like a briefcase. It looked like she was still shaken up by the electrical shocks. Shoulders hunched, head lowered, she shivered once or twice, even though it was a mild day.

Then, from the corner of my eye, I noticed a motion. The scruffy guy we'd been watching saw Una too—and he wasn't idly loitering anymore. Snapping to attention, he began to walk toward her with determined strides.

Una's head jerked up, and her step faltered. Already he was only about ten yards away from her. Cringing backward against the nearest car for safety, she yelled, "Leave me alone! Go away!"

The young man did not stop. In fact, he hurried toward Una even faster.

George and I were at the other end of the parking lot, but we started to run toward them. As if in slow motion, I saw Raggedy Man stretch his arms out toward Una, ready to grab her. Una wailed and threw her arms over her head, but he managed to catch her arm.

As loudly as I could, I shouted, "Let her go!"

10

A Stalker Lurks

When someone's up to no good, they don't hang around waiting to find out why you're shouting at them. Without even looking in our direction, the guy dropped Una's arms and raced away from us. He was fast as a cat. Before we got to Una's side, he had plunged into the tall weeds and vanished.

"Are you okay?" I asked Una.

She nodded, looking dazed. "You're . . . the saboteurs from Salle Budapest. Why are you still here?"

"You explain, George." I had no time to waste. "And have Charlie get my car running—I'll be back!" I dashed off in pursuit of Una's scruffy attacker.

Only a few feet from the edge of the parking lot, I was swallowed up in an urban jungle. The acreage behind Salle Olympique had probably been farmland at one time, but it was overgrown with tall grass, fast-sprouting trees, and big, tough weeds—not to mention loads of trash. The ground under my feet was uneven, and I had to use both hands to fight my way through.

The attacker had a head start on me, and like I said, he was fast. My best hope was that his long overcoat would get caught in the tangled underbrush. Only a few yards in, though, I saw his coat, flung into a towering thicket of nettles. Desperate to get away, he'd taken it off—and from the looks of it, he wasn't a guy who could afford to buy a new one. He sure was anxious to escape. That told me one thing: He was feeling guilty about something.

Of course, if he got away, I'd never find out what.

Thick as the undergrowth was, I could spot where he had crashed through ahead of me. But he didn't stay in the weedy lot for long. His trail cut across the corner to a chain-link fence, where there was a gap just big enough for him to squeeze through. He must have known exactly where that hole in the fence was—which told me he knew this neighborhood pretty well.

As I slipped through the fence and ran across the pavement, I remembered to check out my surroundings. I'd gotten lost before, and it wasn't fun. I was behind a bank branch. Running past the drive-up ATM, I came out onto another street.

Which way had he gone? I paused, scanning the street to the right. No sign of him. I looked to the left. No sign. But I did see a woman pulling on the leash of a barking dog, one of those yappy little terriers that wants to hunt every moving thing he sees. The dog was straining to chase something, or someone, that had just disappeared down the mouth of an alley. My instincts told me it wasn't just a stray cat or a squirrel.

I raced across the street, laying on some extra speed to beat the oncoming traffic. I heard a squeal of tires behind me as a driver stomped on the brakes to avoid hitting me. I waved a hand wildly to thank the driver and ran on into the alley.

The guy may have been familiar with the neighborhood, but in his panic he wasn't thinking clearly. This alley had a continuous line of brick wall on either side, the matching backs of two long blocks of stores. Service doors punctuated the walls every twenty yards or so, but they were all locked up tight. It was like an extended chute, with no escape on either side. The asphalt was cracked and creviced; garbage cans and stacks of empty boxes leaned against the walls; fast-food trash, broken bottles, and flattened aluminum cans littered the ground. And at the far end, I could see him, long hair flying and baggy pants bunched around his torn sneakers, running madly. He was close to the place where the alley opened up onto the next street.

But before he made it, a familiar red pickup truck pulled up at that far end of the alley, screeching up onto the sidewalk to block off the guy's escape.

It was Charlie Adams, my knight in shining armor.

Raggedy Man skittered to a stop and whirled around. He saw me coming up behind him. He knew he had no place else to run, so he scrambled up onto a small Dumpster and tried to scale the wall. Of course, the building was three stories high. No way would he get over it.

By then Charlie and I had reached the Dumpster. The runner sank onto its lid. "Okay, I give up," he moaned.

"Get down from there," I demanded. "Tell me who you are and why you were trying to hurt that girl at the fencing studio."

The young man cringed, hopped off the Dumpster, and looked up like a scared dog. "I would never hurt Una!"

"You know her?"

He hung his head. "Yeah, I know her," he muttered.

"So you were lurking outside the salle, waiting for her?" I asked.

He nodded miserably. "She's my girlfriend."

That was a shocker. "She didn't act like a girl meeting her boyfriend," I said.

He sighed. "All right, she's not my girlfriend anymore. She was, but . . . we broke up, a couple of months ago." His pale face twitched with a painful memory. Then he looked at me, eyes blazing with passion. He really did have nice blue eyes, I had to admit, now that I was close enough to see them. "It's all because of her dad! He broke us up. He doesn't think I'm right for Una. He wants her to focus on college, on becoming a fencing champion. And he thinks I distract her."

"Let me guess—you're not a college student," I said.

He shook his head. "I dropped out a year ago, to pursue my music instead. I'm in a rock band—the Sinners Syndicate." He pushed back his long hair, and suddenly I saw his ratty clothes in a completely different way—like a rock-and-roll wardrobe instead of a homeless vagrant's tatters.

"The Sinners Syndicate?" Charles repeated. "I've seen posters for your concerts. What's your name? What do you play?"

"I'm Doug Calley," he replied, trying to look modest, although it was plain he was pleased to be recognized. "I'm the lead guitarist, plus I write most of the songs. We've been getting more gigs lately, and when I'm on the road I miss too many classes. It's a waste of money to pay tuition if you don't go to class. But Una's dad didn't see it that way. Yes, I'm really getting somewhere with the music, but that's not good enough for his daughter."

"And how does Una feel about that?" I asked, feeling sympathy for Raggedy Man all of a sudden.

Doug frowned. "I don't know for sure. She seemed pretty upset when he broke us up, but she went along with it. She's refused to see me ever since. She won't take my phone calls, she won't answer the letters I've written. I thought if she saw me face-to-face, she might feel differently."

"So that's why you were at the fencing meet on Tuesday," I guessed.

Doug nodded. "But that was no good—her dad was there. I should have known; he goes to all her tournaments. And then I saw her get injured, which was upsetting."

I remembered seeing Doug in the crowd surrounding Una during the suspension of her bout with DeLyn. It was true, he did look upset then.

"But you were hanging around Salle Budapest a week ago," I recalled, "the first time I saw you. Why Salle Budapest? Una doesn't fence there."

Doug screwed his mouth to one side. "Well, I'd

heard through the grapevine that she was dating somebody else—another fencer. That worried me. Her dad would love her to have a fencing boyfriend. So I went to River Heights to check out this guy, Damon Brittany."

"Damon?" Doug must have gotten his facts wrong. From the nasty comments I'd heard Damon make about Una, I'd say she was the last girl in the world he'd date.

Doug nodded. "I saw him with Una at a college meet, and he sure looked interested. But that day in River Heights, he left fencing class with another girl—a tall African-American girl. They looked pretty connected."

"That was his twin sister, DeLyn," I informed Doug.

"You're kidding!" He frowned. "So he doesn't have a new girlfriend?"

"If he does, it's not her. But I don't think it's Una, either."

Doug looked relieved. "So I still have a chance?"

"Una didn't exactly welcome you with open arms back there," I pointed out. "Any girl would be creeped out by having a guy stalking her."

"I'm not stalking her!"

"I'm sorry, but that's exactly what you're doing," I said. "And you could get arrested for it. She could even have a judge issue a restraining order."

Doug winced. "Really?"

"Absolutely. So take my advice—stop lurking outside the salle. Find another way to win Una back."

"I think it's cool that this rock musician is pining away for Una," George said. "But can you imagine, he thought Damon was dating Una? Impossible. Damon can't stand Una."

I looked over at George as we drove back to River Heights. "I know, crazy, huh? Well, I wish Doug and Una good luck. But if he's not a suspect anymore, we're further than ever from solving this case. What's more, we're suspects ourselves now, at least in Paul Mourbiers's eyes."

I had been thinking. I hated the fact that Bela praised George to her face, only to put her down behind her back. I couldn't let him get away with that. "George, I was just wondering—whenever Bela tells you how great you are, isn't DeLyn usually nearby?"

"Well, yes—why?"

"Well, you know how coaches play mind games with their athletes. I wonder if Bela might not be . . . let's say, exaggerating your ability, to motivate DeLyn."

Immediately I wished I had kept quiet. George's

mouth dropped open, and her eyes filled with tears. "What? Are you saying I'm not a talented fencer? Are you saying Bela lied to me? Nancy, I've never known you to act jealous like this."

Jealous? Was she kidding?

I could feel the heat of George's anger in the seat beside me. Luckily, we were getting close to her house. I apologized, but George still seemed furious when she got out of the car. She sure slammed the car door harder than usual. And she didn't even look back as she strode into the house.

All the way back home, I felt lousy. Yes, my intentions had been good. All I'd wanted was to open George's eyes. But the way she saw it, I was ruining her new passion. How could I do that to one of my best friends?

As I pulled up to my house, I saw something that drove all thoughts of our fight right out of my mind.

Something was sticking out of the front door of our house.

I pulled my car up the drive, parked, and jumped out, scarcely believing what I saw.

A sword was sticking into the wooden door, the afternoon sunlight playing off its gleaming blade.

The point had been stabbed through a stiff white fencing gauntlet, just like the one Una had worn at the meet on Tuesday. And like Una's gauntlet, it had

119

a dark red bloodstain on the cuff. That red stain dribbled down the door.

On top of the glove, held in place by the sword, was a note, scrawled in thick black letters. THIS IS WHAT HAPPENS TO BUSYBODIES.

11

More Than a Threat

That naked sword, slashing my front door, was unsettling, all right. But it wasn't the first anonymous threat I'd received in my career as a detective—and it probably wouldn't be the last. If you want to scare off Nancy Drew, you have to try a lot harder than that.

In fact, I thought grimly as I yanked the sword out of the door, getting a threat always makes me more determined than ever to solve a case. I also see it as a sign that I'm getting close to a solution. Not that I felt anywhere close, but obviously someone was nervous about getting caught.

Now if I could only figure out who.

This was a time when three heads would be better than one. As soon as I went inside, I phoned Bess and Ned and asked them to come over to help. Normally

I would have called George, too. Four heads are even better than three. But I just didn't feel I could call George right then.

"Didn't George say there's a college fencing meet tomorrow?" Bess asked as we sat around the kitchen table, eating the dinner Hannah had cooked for us.

"Yup," I said. "It's tomorrow."

"That's a perfect opportunity for the saboteur to strike again," Bess said.

"We've got to be one step ahead of them," said Ned. "We can't wait to let somebody else get hurt."

I nodded. "Why don't we make a list of our main suspects? Then we can divide them among us and monitor their activities tomorrow. As soon as we see them doing anything suspicious, we can step in."

"Good idea." Ned picked up a notepad and a pencil.

"Top of the list is Paul Mourbiers," Bess said.

Ned nodded as he wrote. "And right below him, Bela Kovacs."

Bess frowned. "Do you still have it in for him, Ned?"

"No, Ned's right—Bela is a suspect," I said. "I know his salle has suffered from the bad publicity, but who knows—he may have some ulterior motive for damaging his own business. He hasn't been physically hurt, and he's had access to just about every place where there's been sabotage."

"Except for Salle Olympique today," Bess pointed out.

"True, but at this point, we can't get hung up on making every incident fit into the pattern," I said. "Some may be simple coincidences. The defective lamé plug could have just been worn out."

"Here's another possibility," Ned said. "What if Una damaged her own lamé on purpose, to throw us off the scent?"

"That's possible," I agreed. "I don't see how she could have damaged the equipment at Salle Budapest—she'd be recognized if she showed up there—but write her down as a suspect."

"And what about Doug Calley?" Bess asked. "His story about being Una's old boyfriend is very romantic, but who knows what he'd do to get her back?"

"How would sabotaging both fencing salles help Doug Calley win Una back?" I wondered.

"He could show he supports her fencing career by hurting her rivals," Bess pointed out.

"At the risk of hurting Una heself? Remember, she's been hit twice by the sabotage."

Bess looked thoughtful. "I see your point. Maybe it's just that he's mad at her—mad enough to hurt her. Being rejected can turn any love ugly."

"Okay," I said. "Add him to the list."

"What about Damon and DeLyn?" Ned asked, jotting down Calley's name.

I frowned. "Both of them have been hurt by the sabotage, but like you said, Ned, someone could stage an incident to hurt themselves, just to divert suspicion."

"Or sometimes an act of sabotage backfires," Ned said. "Suppose, for example, that DeLyn set up that incident at the tournament to hurt Una. She wouldn't expect to be disqualified as a result."

"Or suppose Damon put on DeLyn's mask by mistake——," I began, when the doorbell rang. "Hmmm, wonder who that could be?"

Believe me, I was surprised—and relieved—when I opened my front door and saw George. "Hey, Nancy," she said hesitantly. "Okay if I come in?"

"Sure!" I said. "We're talking over the case, and we could use your insight. Have you eaten yet?"

George inhaled. "Well, yes, but—is that Hannah's roast chicken? I guess I could manage a second helping."

I grinned. "Come on in."

"I wanted to apologize, too," George said. "I went home and thought about it. I was wrong to accuse you of being jealous. Why would you be jealous of my fencing? You don't care about fencing."

"I shouldn't have told you all that stuff, though," I said. "Maybe Bela really does think you are good— who am I to say?"

George sighed. "Nancy, I have to face facts. I lost my bout on Tuesday, and today Mourbiers easily parried my moves and scored lots of touches on me. The only person who ever says I'm good is Bela—and you're right, he has reasons for deluding me. What he really cares about is his champion, DeLyn. I'm nowhere near her level." She shook her head. "No, I have a long way to go to become a decent fencer. This sport takes years of training—look how long DeLyn has been at it! I'll probably never be as good as her. Even Damon isn't as good as she is, and he's been fencing longer than she has."

"You could still be a good fencer without being as good as DeLyn," I said. "Don't set your standards too high."

George smiled and put her arm through mine. "And if I never turn out to be any good, so be it," she said. "But I still care about the salle and my friends there. So what are we waiting for? Let's solve this case!"

"There has been one new development," I told George as we walked into the kitchen. "I found this stuck in my front door, with this note attached."

George gave a low whistle as she looked at the sword. "That's a saber," she noted.

"Is it?" Ned said. "Where would you get that kind of a sword?"

George looked up at him, thinking. "Well—not

every fencer would own a saber. You'd only have one if you specialized in saber bouts." She hesitated. "Damon and DeLyn are both saber fighters."

I felt my stomach sinking. Everywhere we turned on this case, it kept circling back to DeLyn Brittany. The first act of sabotage was at her match on Tuesday. Her foil was missing its safety tip. Her brother had nearly been overcome by ammonia fumes. It was her rival, Una, who had been shocked by faulty wiring today.

And then, in a flash of intuition, I took the same facts and put them into a different pattern. A pattern where DeLyn was the victim, not the perpetrator. Someone else had wanted her bout on Tuesday to go wrong. Someone else had hoped she'd fence with a naked foil and hurt others. Someone else had caused DeLyn's rival to get an electric shock.

And those ammonia fumes—they had been on DeLyn's mask in the first place. Even if someone else ended up breathing them.

Suddenly it came to me in a flash. "It's Damon," I said.

George seemed shocked. "Damon? No way, Nancy! Damon would never hurt his own salle—or his own sister. He loves DeLyn."

I shook my head stubbornly. "Damon has had the opportunity to commit every act of sabotage so far—except for this morning, and we really don't know how or when that lamé was damaged, do we?"

"Opportunity, yes," Bess admitted, "but where's his motive? Like you always tell us, Nancy, no one commits a crime without a motive."

"I agree that he loves his sister and he wouldn't physically hurt her. But he might hurt her another way—by messing up her fencing career. He's jealous of her success. Even though it makes him feel lousy, he can't help it. After all, he took up fencing first, and now she's the star. Even his scholarship may be due to her."

Bess shook her head. "But what motive would he have for hurting Una? If he wants to get back at his sister, hurting her main rival wouldn't do it."

George and I traded glances. "Doug Calley told us he'd heard that Damon and Una were dating," George suggested. "My first reaction was, no way. From what I've heard him say, he can't stand her. But now I wonder . . ."

I was starting to wonder too. It seemed like none of us really knew Damon Brittany. We had no idea what made him tick—or what he was capable of doing.

And that could be very dangerous.

Walking into the field house the next morning, we were the first spectators through the door. I nudged

Bess. "Look—the TV station sent a crew again."

"Maybe this is the follow-up Derrick promised," Bess said hopefully.

I frowned. "That's not Derrick over there—it's Kelly Chaffetz again. Hoping to get a repeat of Tuesday's excitement on camera, I'll bet."

"You can't blame her," Ned said. "Bela blew his chance at getting some positive spin when he sent the TV crew away from the salle on Wednesday. Kelly Chaffetz won't pass up the opportunity to get some more juicy footage for tonight's show. It's all about the ratings, you know."

"Well, she won't get anything juicy if I have anything to do with it," I said. "That's what we're here to prevent. Ned you find Damon, and don't let him out of your sight. He's probably in the men's locker room. I'll keep my eyes open for any kind of sabotage in the women's locker room. I wish we'd been able to get in here earlier. Too bad you weren't fencing today, George."

"Can't help it if I'm not on the college team," George said. "And the way I'm fencing, I don't expect a scholarship in my future either." She gave me a rueful smile. "Bess and I will stay out here. I'll find Bela and stick to him like a burr. Bess, you follow Paul Mourbiers—at least he won't recognize you."

128

I completely ignored the sign reading COMPETI-TORS ONLY taped to the locker room door. In the confusion inside, with all the fencers getting into their white tunics and breeches, no one stopped me. Of course, I had intentionally dressed in white clothes so I wouldn't stand out in the fencing crowd.

I smiled and said hi to every girl I passed, and they always smiled back as if they recognized me. I personally have a great memory for faces and names, but most people don't—and they hate to admit it. If you act like they should know you, they pretend they do. And that was enough for me to blend in. I even poked into a few open lockers and equipment bags, pretending they were mine. By now I was familiar with fencing equipment. I knew what was supposed to be in there and what wasn't.

Crouching down between two rows of lockers, I couldn't see the locker room entrance. But when a tense hush fell over the room, I figured someone important had just arrived. I crept to the end of the lockers and peered around. Una had just walked in, head high, looking as nonchalant as possible. Right behind her was DeLyn, also looking as if she had no idea who Una was.

You know who they reminded me of at that moment? Bela Kovacs and Paul Mourbiers. Funny how the arrogant attitudes of the teachers had rubbed off on their students.

Both DeLyn and Una were bound to recognize me and wonder why I was there. But that couldn't be helped—I had to find a way to check their equipment. Waiting until Una's back was turned, I walked boldly out into the main aisle. "Hi, DeLyn!" I said.

DeLyn's eyes opened wide in surprise, but she didn't give me away. "Hi," she replied.

"Say, do you have an extra foil I could borrow?" I asked, keeping up the pretense that I was a fencer.

She shoved her bag toward me with her toe as she strapped on her tunic. "Bela fixed my foil for me—it's in there. And I'm not fencing foil today, only saber."

I knelt down and began to check her equipment. "You have all your sabers?" I asked, thinking about the sword that had been stuck in my door.

She looked perplexed. "Yes, why?"

"No reason." I picked up her gauntlet and tested the seams, then checked the electrical plug on both of the lamés she had brought.

Just then Una came cruising past DeLyn, her mask under one arm, a saber cocked jauntily in her gloved hand. "Better get a move on, DeLyn," she said, tossing her words coolly over one shoulder as she passed by. "We're paired for our first bout, and it starts in three minutes. You don't want to forfeit again."

"You'd better hope I do—it's your only chance of winning," DeLyn shot back. I stole a glance at DeLyn. She didn't look half as confident as her words made her sound.

"Better get out there," I murmured to DeLyn. Seeing Una's equipment bag sitting on the floor, I scooted over to it. None of the other fencers noticed me unzipping the bag and slipping my hand inside.

A foil, a spare gauntlet, an extra saber—the usual equipment. I pulled out a wrapped-up cube of rosin, which I knew fencers rub into their shoes to ensure good traction on the mat. A small box of Band-Aids and antiseptic ointment, in case of blisters or scrapes, I imagined. Or another sword scratch. I remembered that saber bouts were different from foil bouts. Saber fencers can score a touch on a much greater area of the body—the thighs and arms as well as the torso—and can score touches with the side of the blade, not just the tip. Saber fencers have a much greater chance of getting gouged. It takes nerves of steel to fence saber.

I thrust my hand into Una's bag one more time and hit a small, hard glass object, about three inches high. I pulled it out. It was a brown glass medicine bottle, with a yellowing label from a local pharmacy. Inside was a colorless sort of crystalline powder. I scanned the label curiously.

My heart skipped a beat.

According to the label, this was a bottle of strych-nine.

Have you ever seen anybody die of strychnine poisoning? I bet not. I have been told it's one of the most gruesome deaths possible—every muscle in the body arcing in endless spasms and convulsions, the face contorting in a horrible grimace, until eventually, the victim dies of sheer exhaustion. I did not want to see my first strychnine death today.

Clutching the deadly bottle in my hand, I jumped up, grabbed the bag by its handles, and raced out of the locker room, heading for the fencing area. My heart was hammering and my blood was roaring in my ears.

Across the field house floor, I spotted Una's tall, slim figure advancing down the mat, saber in hand, against DeLyn. Una's arm rose, saber glinting. She lunged toward DeLyn and slashed her sword down-ward in a long diagonal stroke. DeLyn yelped and twisted away, her gloved hand rising to her cheek.

I gasped. Una had just grazed DeLyn's cheek with the edge of her saber.

And if Una's blade was coated with strychnine powder . . . DeLyn could die!

12

Find the Motive

I **ran to the fencing** strip, with Una's bag banging against my legs. Out of the corner of my eye I noticed someone else running toward the mat from another direction—Damon. And Ned was not far behind.

Damon reached the strip first. "Referee, inspect that fencer's sword!" he demanded, pointing at Una.

Una stood, seething, on the mat, her sword dangling at her side. The TV cameraman was heading our way. And I could see Bela and Mourbiers both striding toward the mat.

"And go through her equipment bag, too!" Damon added.

"Damon, what are you doing?" DeLyn protested. "I'm fine—it's just a scratch."

The referee frowned. He wasn't the same official who'd overseen the girls' bout on Tuesday, but he clearly knew the history of Una and DeLyn's rivalry. "Where is your equipment bag?" he asked Una.

"In the locker room," she began, "but—"

"No, it isn't—I've got it here!" I announced, holding up Una's bag. The referee gave me a curious look. I couldn't see Una's face under the mask, but I guess she was perplexed too. I didn't bother to explain—there was no time to waste.

I glanced nervously at DeLyn. The scratch on her cheek wasn't deep—but you don't need much of a laceration for strychnine to work inside the body. Reaction to strychnine starts ten to twenty minutes after exposure, beginning with a stiff neck and shoulders. A victim's chance of survival is much greater if you begin treatment before the symptoms start. I wasn't going to wait for the referee to finish searching the bag.

"What did you expect they'd find, Damon—this?" I asked. I held up the medicine bottle.

Damon jerked back, startled. "Wha—"

"The label says this is strychnine," I said as quietly as possible to the referee, throwing a nervous look over my shoulder at the TV camera behind us. Ned, reading my mind, stepped in front of the camera so the cameraman had to shut it off.

"I found it in Una's bag a few minutes ago," I went on. "I don't know why it's there—but if she put this on her saber blade, DeLyn needs her stomach pumped right away. Once the strychnine gets into her system—"

"Did I just hear something about my baby needing her stomach pumped?" asked Mrs. Brittany, thrusting her arms wide as she marched through the crowd. "What is in that bottle, Miss Drew? Damon, what do you know about this?"

How had she heard me? Oh well. "Damon, you put that bottle in Una's bag, didn't you?" I asked.

Damon flinched—and then nodded reluctantly.

Mrs. Brittany gasped. "Why, Damon, why would you want to hurt your sister?"

Damon raised his hands, pleading. "Hurt DeLyn? Never! Sheesh, there's nothing in that bottle—just some bath salts."

I felt an enormous sense of relief—DeLyn was safe! But it was time to bring Damon to account. "Then why does the label say strychnine?" I asked him. "And why did you put it in Una's bag?"

The referee crossed his arms. "Look, we have a fencing bout to complete here. If this injury isn't serious, we should get on with it. You folks discuss this elsewhere."

Damon threw his arms up and stalked off through

the crowd. But I wasn't going to let him get away—and neither was Bela Kovacs. We were right behind him. Ned, Bess, and George followed us. So did Paul Mourbiers and Mrs. Brittany. A crowd of curious onlookers trailed after us, including Kelly Chaffetz and the cameraman, although their camera was still turned off. There was another guy there who looked familiar, but I couldn't quite place him—a thin young man with a brown ponytail, dressed in a neat polo shirt and khakis. He kept clenching and unclenching his fists and glaring at Damon, as if he wanted to take him apart.

At the edge of the fencing floor, Bela grabbed Damon's arm and spun him around. "What are you up to, Damon?" Bela demanded. "If you are behind all this mischief—it could ruin my business—" Bela's face twisted suddenly. "After all I have done for you! I have loved you like my own son."

Damon swallowed, his face sorrowful. "I never meant to hurt the salle, Bela. It was just—I had to get back at Una. How could she break up with me?"

"You mean all of this is . . . over a girl?" Bela looked confounded.

Damon hung his head. "I knew you wouldn't like it, Bela—me dating a Salle Olympique girl. We went out for a couple of months, but I kept it from you. Then last week she broke it off. Some old boyfriend—a guy her father didn't like—she said she couldn't get over him."

The skinny young man in khakis gasped, then grinned. That's when I realized who it was—Doug Calley. He had cleaned up a lot since yesterday. Maybe he had finally realized that that creepy stalker routine was no way to win a girl.

"I had to get back at Una," Damon repeated in a stubborn voice.

"So you sabotaged her equipment?" I guessed.

He nodded sullenly. "On Tuesday, before the bout. I ripped open a gauntlet and peeled the coating off the wires on her lamé. Then I put that faked-up poison bottle in her bag. I didn't want her to get hurt— I just wanted her to get into trouble with the referees for improper equipment. Maybe she'd lose a bout— that would serve her right."

"But it was DeLyn who ended up losing Tuesday's bout," Bess said.

Damon kicked the steel foot of the bleachers. "Yeah, that backfired. But that was because Mourbiers tricked you into losing your temper, Bela."

"I did not—he lost his own temper!" Bela protested.

Damon didn't look like he believed that. "He knew just what to say to get you going, Bela. And all because the TV crew was there, filming it. That's what hurt your business, Bela—not anything I did."

Bela frowned. "But if you hadn't damaged the gauntlet—"

Damon brushed that fact aside with a wave of his hand. "When I saw the effects of that—people canceling their lessons, the bank breathing down your neck—well, that made me fighting mad. I decided to beat Mourbiers at his own game. I'd heard you accuse him of sabotaging the bout, so I decided to make it look like he really was sabotaging your business."

"So that's why you tampered with the equipment at Salle Budapest?" I said. "Removing the sword tips, putting the ampoule of smelling salts inside DeLyn's mask—"

Damon looked surprised that I'd figured that out. "I intended to pull it off of DeLyn before the fumes overcame her. But somehow our masks got switched—I think George did it accidentally."

George flushed. "Now that you mention it, I did hand DeLyn her mask that evening . . . at least I thought it was hers. . . ."

Damon shook his head in disgust. "And all along, there you were, Nancy, pretending to be a friend, when you were really a detective, snooping on us."

"Bela asked me to," I told Damon. "I was hoping to help the salle."

"You knew, somehow—and that's why you stuck your saber in her door," Bess concluded.

"Well, you can clear off now, Nancy," Damon said. "There's nothing to investigate. No one has been hurt, outside of a few minor scratches."

"You're wrong there, Damon," said another man, pushing through the cluster of onlookers. Wearing a university sweatshirt and carrying a clipboard, he was clearly the coach of Damon and DeLyn's college fencing team. "Something has been hurt by all this mischief," he said gravely. "The integrity of fencing. This isn't a sport where people do things like damaging other athletes' equipment. I'm very disappointed in you."

"But coach—" Damon began.

"I am your coach no longer. As of now, you are suspended from the school's team. I will notify the financial aid office that your scholarship has been revoked." He threw a withering glance at Bela Kovacs. "I suppose you can permit Damon to compete for your salle. But I must say, I expected you would have taught him more honor, Bela." The college coach strode away.

"Oh, Damon, baby," Mrs. Brittany exclaimed. "What a shame. How dare he do that to you?"

To my surprise, Damon just shrugged—and almost seemed to smile. "Mama, he was going to kick me off the team soon anyway. I guess I was hoping this would happen. Now at last I can quit fencing."

Bela began to tremble with emotion. "Quit fencing? How can you do that, after all the years you have devoted to it?"

Damon looked pleadingly at his coach and mentor. "Bela, this is DeLyn's sport, not mine. Why haven't any of you figured that out? Haven't you seen how unhappy it makes me? As long as I fence, I will always be in my sister's shadow. I need to find something of my own. Maybe it'll be another sport, or maybe it'll be music, or painting, or science, or politics. But it's got to be mine."

To my left, I heard the TV camera whir, and I jerked around, determined to stop Kelly and her crew from prying into Damon's disgrace. But to my surprise, the scene they were filming was one I never thought would happen—Paul Mourbiers and Bela Kovacs, throwing their arms open and enfolding each other in a huge bear hug.

"After a public altercation on Tuesday, fencing masters Bela Kovacs and Paul Mourbiers have reconciled," Kelly Chaffetz was saying into her microphone. "Let's have a word with these two and see why they agreed to bury the hatchet—or, in this case, the saber."

Paul Mourbiers grinned into the camera. "We may

have our deefferences," he said, his French accent mysteriously stronger than ever, "but thees passion we have for fencing, we hold eet in common."

"We both come out of a great Old World tradition," Bela chimed in. "We love to win, yes, but more than that, we love and honor our sport. And who understands that better than my friend Paul Mourbiers?"

"Of Salle Olympique, in Cutler Falls," Mourbiers sneaked in a plug for his studio.

"*Mon ami*, you will always be welcome at Salle Budapest, here in River Heights," Bela added his own mini-commercial.

"After all that has happened, how can they call each other friends?" Bess whispered in my ear. "Were they faking it all along?"

I thought back on everything I'd heard Bela say about Mourbiers. I didn't think he was that skillful an actor. He'd meant what he said, all right. But he looked like he meant what he was saying now, too.

Ned, beside me, chuckled. "Those two old guys," he said. "They've known each other for so many years—they probably understand each other better than anybody else does."

I nodded, looking at them standing arm in arm, hamming it up for the camera. "That feud of theirs is probably the deepest relationship either one of them has," I said. "Without it they'd be nothing."

Just then, applause burst out from the fencing floor. I turned to look over my shoulder. DeLyn had taken off her mask and was saluting Una. The numbers on the electronic scoring device showed fifteen touches for DeLyn, against six for Una. She had won her bout—fair and square this time.

And Una? I would have thought she'd be upset. But she was barely even looking at DeLyn. She was smiling over at somebody in the nearby bleachers— Doug Calley, with his new look. Maybe at last her dad would approve of Doug and let them get back together.

"Look at DeLyn—how happy she seems," George murmured. "Considering that ten minutes ago she thought her brother was trying to poison her."

"That's what makes her a true champion," I said. "When she's engrossed in doing the thing she loves, she shuts out everything else."

"Kind of like someone I know when she's solving a mystery," Bess said.

Ned grinned. "You mean Nancy Drew, the champion of detectives?"

Bess nodded. "Touché!"

Have you read
the first four books about

**Don't miss *Witch's Sister*
and *Witch Water*
by Phyllis Reynolds Naylor**

"The reader is left with a tingling
uncertainty as to whether Lynn's
fears are the product of an active
imagination or a sharp eye."
—*Booklist*

"An absorbingly scary novel."
—*Publishers Weekly*

"A chilling climax at midnight . . ."
—*Kirkus Reviews*

"The plot is well crafted
with a genuine aura of evil."
—*School Library Journal*

terrifying Mrs. Tuggle?

The saga continues with
The Witch Herself and *The Witch's Eye*
by Phyllis Reynolds Naylor

"The fright quotient rises as
Lynn sneaks about. . . ."
—*Kirkus Reviews*

"Spine-tingling . . . good,
spooky fun."
—*Publishers Weekly*

Think it would be fun to get stuck on a deserted island with the guy you sort of like? Well, try adding the girl who gets on your nerves big-time (*and* who's crushing on the same guy), the bossiest kid in school, your annoying little brother, and a bunch of other people, all of whom have their own ideas about how things should be done. Oh, and have I mentioned that there's no way off this island, and no one knows where you are?

Still sound great? Didn't think so.

Now all I have to worry about is getting elected island leader, finding something to wear for a dance (if you can believe that), and surviving a hurricane, all while keeping *my* crush away from Little Miss Priss. Oh, and one other teeny-tiny little thing: surviving.

Get me outta here!

Read all the books in the Castaways trilogy:

#1 Worst Class Trip Ever

#2 Weather's Here, Wish You Were Great

#3 Isle Be Seeing You

REDISCOVER THE CLASSIC MYSTERIES OF NANCY DREW

$5.99 ($8.99 CAN) each
AVAILABLE AT YOUR LOCAL BOOKSTORE OR LIBRARY

Grosset & Dunlap • A division of Penguin Young Readers Group
A member of Penguin Group (USA), Inc. • A Pearson Company
www.penguin.com/youngreaders

star power

by Catherine Hapka

She's beautiful, she's talented, she's famous.

She's a star!

Things would be perfect
if only her family
was around to help
her celebrate. . . .

Follow the
adventures of
fourteen-year-old
pop star
Star Calloway

HAVE YOU READ ALL OF THE ALICE BOOKS?

PHYLLIS REYNOLDS NAYLOR

STARTING WITH ALICE
Atheneum Books for
  Young Readers
  0-689-84395-X
Aladdin Paperbacks
  0-689-84396-8

ALICE IN BLUNDERLAND
Atheneum Books for
  Young Readers
  0-689-84397-6

LOVINGLY ALICE
Atheneum Books for
  Young Readers
  0-689-84399-2

THE AGONY OF ALICE
Atheneum Books for
  Young Readers
  0-689-31143-5
Aladdin Paperbacks
  0-689-81672-3

ALICE IN RAPTURE,
  SORT-OF
Atheneum Books for
  Young Readers
  0-689-31466-3
Aladdin Paperbacks
  0-689-81687-1

RELUCTANTLY ALICE
Atheneum Books for
  Young Readers
  0-689-31681-X
Aladdin Paperbacks
  0-689-81688-X

ALL BUT ALICE
Atheneum Books for
Young Readers
  0-689-31773-5
Aladdin Paperbacks
  0-689-85044-1

ALICE IN APRIL
Atheneum Books for
  Young Readers
  0-689-31805-7
Aladdin Paperbacks
  0-689-81686-3

ALICE IN-BETWEEN
Atheneum Books for
  Young Readers
  0-689-31890-0
Aladdin Paperbacks
  0-689-81685-5

ALICE THE BRAVE
Atheneum Books for
  Young Readers
  0-689-80095-9
Aladdin Paperbacks
  0-689-80598-5

ALICE IN LACE
Atheneum Books for
  Young Readers
  0-689-80358-3
Aladdin Paperbacks
  0-689-80597-7

OUTRAGEOUSLY ALICE
Atheneum Books for
  Young Readers
  0-689-80354-0
Aladdin Paperbacks
  0-689-80596-9

ACHINGLY ALICE
Atheneum Books for
  Young Readers
  0-689-80533-9
Aladdin Paperbacks
  0-689-80595-0
Simon Pulse
  0-689-86396-9

ALICE ON THE OUTSIDE
Atheneum Books for
  Young Readers
  0-689-80359-1
Simon Pulse
  0-689-80594-2

GROOMING OF ALICE
Atheneum Books for
  Young Readers
  0-689-82633-8
Simon Pulse
  0-689-84618-5

ALICE ALONE
Atheneum Books for
  Young Readers
  0-689-82634-6
Simon Pulse
  0-689-85189-8

SIMPLY ALICE
Atheneum Books for
  Young Readers
  0-689-84751-3
Simon Pulse
  0-689-85965-1

PATIENTLY ALICE
Atheneum Books for
  Young Readers
  0-689-82636-2
Simon Pulse
  0-689-87073-6

INCLUDING ALICE
Atheneum Books for
  Young Readers
  0-689-82637-0